Books by Jane O'Brien

The White Pine Trilogy:
The Tangled Roots of Bent Pine Lodge #1
The Dunes & Don'ts Antiques Emporium #2
The Kindred Spirit Bed & Breakfast #3

The Lighthouse Trilogy:
The 13th Lighthouse #1
The Painted Duck #2
Owl Creek #3

The Unforgettables
Ruby & Sal #1

Ruby

and

Sal

Connect with Jane O'Brien

www.authorjaneobrien.com

http://www.amazon.com/author/obrienjane

www.facebook.com/janeobrien.author/

Contact: authorjaneobrien@gmail.com

Table of Contents

I'm a kind person; I'm kind to everyone, but if you are unkind to me, then kindness is not what you'll remember me for.

Al Capone

Part One --

Endings

Chapter One

Ivy stood outside the door of the nursing home and waited. She waited for her spinning head to clear. She waited for her breathing to even out. She waited for her hands to stop shaking. It happened each time she came here – the heart palpitations and shortness of breath. She wondered if she would ever get over the feeling of loss when there was no loss as of yet. Each and every time she needed to give herself a pep talk before she went in. "I'm a grown woman. I can handle this. I can do it." Then she took a deep breath, and putting her own feelings of hopelessness aside, she placed one foot in front of the other and walked in.

The lobby was bright and cheerful. Fall decorations of leaves and mums lined the bulletin board, announcing the week's activities; Crochet and

Knitting Club on Monday at 9:30; Bingo on Tuesday and Thursday at 3:00; a Sing-a-long in the cafeteria at 2:00 on Wednesday; Wheelchair Volleyball on Friday at 10 a.m., and a Fish-fry on Friday at 5 p.m. All-in-all it was a wonderful place. Gone were the odorous smells of old-folks homes as in days past. This home smelled like soap and air freshener. The nurses and aides were always smiling, happily bringing cheer to each room as they entered. They called each patient 'honey' or 'sweetie' and never seemed to tire of helping those in need. In Ivy's opinion they were God's angels on Earth.

Ivy walked the hallway toward room 206 and she greeted each person she passed. Some were in wheelchairs, while others moved slowly with walkers, most likely getting in the required steps for the day. She greeted Mrs. Moore who blew her a kiss each time she, or anyone else, passed by. Then there was Mr. Barnes, a long-time resident, who always asked her the score of the Detroit Lions game, even when it was no longer football season. A few residents didn't seem to know where they were at all; they sat quietly in a perpetual doze, wrapped in blankets as their heads lolled forward. But no matter what the level of alertness, each resident was treated with respect and given the dignity they deserved after living a long life, and being contributing members to society.

Ivy stopped in front of the door she was seeking, took a deep breath, and with a quick knock, entered. Her grandmother was in a tilt-back chair, watching game shows, her feet propped up on the raised footstool. Ivy always felt awkward at this point, not wanting to disturb her grandmother's TV. How she longed for the days when her Nana's face would light up as she entered the room. "Hello, Dear. How was your day?" she would say every day after school. And then later, "Ivy, darling. How are you? Is everything okay at work? Tell me about it." Her never-ending patience as she listened to Ivy's tales and woes always amazed her. Since she was an only child and her mother had died at a young age, her grandmother, a widow already, had moved in and helped her father raise her. Olivia had become a mother and a grandmother all rolled up into one. Maybe, Ivy often thought, if she hadn't had so much attention showered upon her, she wouldn't feel so angry at times at how things were now. She had chastised herself many times about her disappointment in her grandmother. 'How dare she, leave me like this, with no one to talk to except GG,' she would think, but immediately after, she would feel selfish and immature.

Olivia Morton was Ivy's grandmother on her father's side. Her father, Thomas, was living in Los Angeles now and rarely came to see his own mother. Ivy understood that he had a job, a new wife, and other children – young children, but she never understood why he ignored his mother the way he did. He said it was too hard, seeing her like this – he couldn't handle it. Well, it was hard on Ivy, too, but someone had to show up once in a while and make sure she was taken care of. So she did what she always did each visit, she put on a big smile, and called out loudly, "Nana, it's me. Ivy. How are you this morning?"

The old woman raised her cloudy grey eyes, and looking straight at Ivy, she said, "Who? Who are you, now?"

A slight frown creased Ivy's forehead. It was difficult for her on the days that her Nana no longer remembered her. Those days used to be few and far between, but lately they were becoming the norm. Ivy was told that her grandmother would lose memory of her altogether on some days, but it would return intermittently, until finally there was no more recognition at all. Each patient was a little different. Alzheimer's could be a fickle disease. Ivy put on a bright smile, and knelt close to her dear, beloved grandmother.

"Nana, I'm your granddaughter. Thomas, your son, is my father. Do you remember Thomas?"

"Oh, Thomas," sighed her grandma. "He's such a nice little boy. A handful, but then most boys are." She chuckled, and Ivy felt good that she was at least happy. "Is Thomas playing outside? I haven't seen him in a few minutes. I need to call him in for lunch."

Tears pricked Ivy's eyes. She took the old woman's hands in her own. "Yes, Nana, he's fine. I'll call him in for you."

"Thank you, miss." And with that, Ivy could see that she had once again lost her grandmother to another time period, an era when she was a happy mother and young wife.

"I'll be right back, okay?" There was no response, as the old woman returned to whatever scene was playing out in her head.

Ivy stepped out in the hall, where she quietly shed her tears, then she walked to the nurses' station. The head nurse, Annie, looked up from her paperwork and greeted her with a smile. "Ivy, it's so good to see you again. I'm sorry I wasn't on duty the last few times you were here."

"No problem, Annie. I'm here often enough that we can stay in touch. Besides, the other nurses and aides have been keeping me informed of any changes."

Annie suddenly had a more solemn look on her face. "You might want to contact her doctor. I'm afraid things are moving more quickly now. We see memory loss more and more each day, and then there's her physical problems. She is in overall good health for an 84-year-old, but the disease is taking its toll. I'm afraid she doesn't have too much time left."

"Yes, I understand. I knew it was coming, but it will still be difficult when that day does happen. I'll have to call my father. He should come home while he can still talk to her." A flash of anger crossed Ivy's face. She could feel her blood pressure rise whenever she thought about her father's behavior towards his own mother. In her opinion, it was disgraceful.

"Well, on a better note," added Annie, "Ruby is fantastic. That woman! She gives us all so much pleasure."

"That's good to know. I'm on my way there next. At least with her, I can have a two-way conversation that makes sense." Ivy's spirits lifted immediately as they always did whenever she thought of GG. "Thanks, Annie, you ladies are wonderful. I'm so happy we found you. I always feel as if you're caring for my loved ones as if they're your own."

"You are most welcome, my dear. It's our privilege. We love each of our residents here at Red Pine. Well, I must get back to work, but if there's anything else I can help you with, I'd be glad to."

"No, no. You've done more than enough. Thank you."

"Have a nice visit with GG, then."

Ivy dreaded the call she would have to make to her father. Talking to him was never pleasant, but it had to done. She was sure he would never ask about his mother if Ivy didn't force him to face what she was going through. And he certainly did not even think about GG. That dear woman! Ivy loved her great-grandmother so much. It was always a pleasure to visit her, so she saved her for last. That way when she left the building she wasn't quite so depressed.

GG, so called because great-grandmother was difficult for a child to say, was a delight. She had recently turned one hundred and one and had always been as active as one that age could possibly be. Mentally, she was as sharp as a tack; nothing slipped by her. GG was very upset when she was told she would have to leave her house and move into a home. After a leg break that would not heal, there was no other alternative. Here at Red Pine, she received the care she needed, but she was also treated with respect. And as she said now, she had never been taken care of so well in her life. Upon Ivy's first visit with her, she proclaimed she was treated like a queen. "Why, Ivy, they make my bed, do my laundry, and cook for me. And I'll never have to do another dish in my life. What more could a girl ask for." Then she giggled at her own joke. Another benefit for Ruby was that she was near her daughter, Olivia, so she was able to visit her every day. They had been lucky that a room was open in the same senior care center, so now the two were just down the hall from each other. And needless to say, it was much easier on Ivy. She could see each of them on the same day, as she did three times a week.

Ivy's steps picked up as she walked down the hall and turned the corner to her GG's room. She could feel her burdens being lifted and her spirits pick up, as she knocked and then opened the door to room 308. GG was sitting on her bed with her bad leg propped up on a pillow, her head of snow white hair bent low as she worked on a crossword puzzle. She had a peaceful smile on her face as she hummed happily to herself. The song sounded to Ivy like 'I Can't Give You Anything But Love, Baby.' Ivy wondered what she was thinking about.

Chapter Two

"Hello, GG. You're looking wonderful today."

The old woman's smile was radiant as soon as she saw her great-granddaughter. "Ivy! I lost track of time. I should have combed my hair a bit."

"You're beautiful as always, GG." Ivy planted a kiss on Ruby's soft cheek and gave her a gentle hug. She had been warned by the doctor that Ruby might be susceptible to bones breaking easily now. To Ivy, her GG seemed like a delicate porcelain doll. Her skin was still creamy, her hair sparkled like white diamonds, and her eyes the color of a light blue Michigan sky in the morning. "How's the crossword coming along?"

"Oh, you know, if they would stick to using words in the dictionary, I'd be fine, but new words appear all the time that I'm not familiar with. Then I have to wing it." She chuckled to herself.

"What kind of words don't you know?"

"How about this one? I only got it because I was able to fill in the other boxes. What in the world is an emoji? It says 'a small digital image used to express emotion.'"

Ivy laughed and pulled out her phone. She tapped on the text window and brought up the long list of emojis. "Look at this. These little pictures are emojis. When you text you can use a picture instead of a word to say what you mean. It's sort of a short cut."

"Oh, for Pete's sake," exclaimed Ruby. "Doesn't anyone know how to write, anymore? My friend Myrtle told me that her great-grandchildren will no longer be learning writing, long-hand is what we called it, but I guess they call it cursive, now. First, they changed the name, and now it's obsolete. What will they do if a machine fails them? Are you telling me, these kids today won't be able to write their own name?"

"I'm afraid so, GG. They learn to print and type and that's it." Ivy sat on the end of the bed next to Ruby. "I'm sad that soon there won't be any documents left with a person's handwriting on it. When I do genealogy, one of the treats is finding a document with my ancestor's signature. I like to run my fingers over it, and see if I can feel a connection to their hand."

"Yes, you're right," said GG. "Old letters and postcards tell such a story. Now it seems that all the young folks only email and text, and then they are deleted when they aren't needed any longer. Don't they realize their past will disappear? I always loved holding a recipe that my mother wrote out. It brought such comfort to see her script. She had a beautiful slant. All the letters were perfect, and very legible."

"I've often wondered how they learned to write like that. How do you make a whole generation of kids have good handwriting?"

"Work, child, work. We spent hours, with our papers at just the right angle, learning to make our letters." Ruby chuckled as she remembered how Miss

Markham made them do O's over and over again. "Of course, we didn't have to learn about computers, and going to space, and world affairs. Subjects were simple then. Readin', 'riting and 'rithmetic, as we called it. Our math was basic, and there wasn't a whole lot to science."

"Tell me more about school when you were young."

"Well, we learned the proper way to address a letter, and of course we always had an etiquette class. It was a one-room school so for some things we could combine the grades. It was the school's business as well as the parents' to teach manners. Quite a bit of time was spent learning the proper way to greet someone, how and when to shake hands – of course ladies didn't shake hands then. Hugging was reserved for close family members only. It was considered bad manners to hug a stranger. How times have changed. Now everyone hugs everyone. It still seems strange to me."

Ivy loved hearing stories of old times, and Ruby loved to tell them. "Did you graduate from high school? I don't think I've ever heard you say."

"Oh no. I was one of the lucky ones, though. My dad let me stay on until the eighth grade. Some kids had to drop out earlier if they had a farm. Kids were required to stay in until they were 14 years old, or at the completion of the eighth grade, whichever came first, but it wasn't enforced. Some of the children had to quit when they were only eleven or twelve. Some never even went to school at all. I was glad I could go to school. I loved reading, and school was my only source for books. The teacher would let me take one from her shelf, and then when I was finished, I could exchange it for another. Soon, though, my father put a stop to it. I would have read all day if he would have let me." GG's breath was getting weaker, and it caused her to pause for a coughing spell.

Ivy handed her the glass of water on the stand next to her chair. Ruby pulled a Kleenex out of her sleeve to wipe her eyes.

"I'm sorry, GG. I believe I've made you talk too much."

As Ruby laughed her face lit up like a spry little elf. "Not too many people could ever make me stop talking. That was one problem I had in school. The teacher always told my ma 'she's a good student but she talks too much.' The only time I ever shut up was – well, that's a story for another time."

"I'm sorry, if I tired you, GG. It's always so much fun to hear your stories. Would you mind if I started to write some of them down? I'm really interested in being a published author someday, and I don't want to lose your history. You've had such a fascinating life."

"Of course, darling. You can write whatever you like. Soon, I won't be here and my past will go with me. I never thought I would live this long. I've out lived two husbands, and all of my friends. I try not to dwell on that too much. I get lonely when I think of it. How's your grandma, by the way? I haven't been down to see her today."

"She's getting worse, I'm afraid. It's so sad. She didn't know me at all today." Ivy tried not to shed tears, but a few escaped anyway.

"It's so difficult to see my own daughter like that. I don't understand why God would give me a perfectly good mind and let hers slip away like that. She only sees me as an old woman who comes to visit her regularly. She hasn't known me as her mother in quite a while. My heart aches for her." Ruby pulled out her Kleenex once again, but this time to wipe tears of sadness.

"I'm sorry to make you sad, GG. At least we can take comfort in knowing that she is happy, even if she is in her own little world."

"Yes, I'm afraid God is going to call her home soon. Then I'll only have you left, Ivy. You won't leave me here all alone, will you?"

"Absolutely not! Never!" Ivy hugged her dear, cherished great-grandmother and held her for a while this time, as she rubbed her back for comfort. Just then an aide stuck her head in the door.

"Ruby, it's time for lunch. Do you need a push to the cafeteria?"

"I think I'll take my food in my room, today, Joan, if you don't mind. I'm a little tired."

"No problem, sweetie. Fill out your order, and we'll bring it to you."

Ivy stood up and gathered her purse and sweater. "Well, GG, I'd better get going. Next time, I'll come at lunchtime and eat with you. How's that?"

"That would be wonderful. You're such a dear girl."

"See you in two days. I love you." Ivy studied her GG's face before she kissed it. She wanted to memorize every detail, every dear precious wrinkle. She didn't know how long she would have her, and photos just weren't enough.

Chapter Three

The keys clinked as they hit the dish by the door. She dropped the tote bag with a decided plop. Next, came the shoes, kicked off and quickly forgotten. No one ever said Ivy was a neat and tidy person. It was one of her biggest flaws and she knew it, but at this stage of her life, she seemed helpless to do anything about it. Try as she might, her apartment always looked like a tornado had just passed through, scattering papers, books, and clothing in the oddest of places. It was a mess, but it was her mess, and she knew right where everything was. In some ways, the disarray gave her a feeling of comfort. In fact, most times, she actually felt cozy in what some would see as turmoil.

Ivy's mother had had a difficult time with it while she was growing up. No matter what amount of chastising, punishment, or cajoling, she could not get her to change her ways. Finally, one day when she was twelve, her mother had closed her bedroom door and never went in again. Ivy was told she would need to place her clothing in the hamper or it would not get washed. Once cleaned, her clothing was neatly folded and strategically placed at the entrance to her room so that Ivy would have to step over it to gain entrance. Ivy would sigh, bend over to pick it up, and place it on the already littered floor by her closet door. Then throughout the week, she would work off the pile as she dressed for school. This method had finally stopped the squabbling between mother and daughter, but her mother had lived in fear that her grandmother or one of the other relatives would one day happen to open the bedroom door and see how Ivy lived.

And true to form, the worst scenario actually happened. Her uncle, who was a very fastidious man, opened the door to her room to call her to dinner, and the whole house could hear him bellow in shock. "Whoa! What is this?" He slammed the door and marched down the hallway to ask her mother what was going on. "I'm teaching her a lesson. Just forget about it. One of these days she'll get embarrassed with her friends and she'll have to clean. Then she'll understand what other people expect of her. Until then, I grin and bear it." But the truth was that never happened, because all of her friends had rooms that were disasters, too. The difference was that when they grew up and had a home of their own and children who required vacuumed carpets and freshly mopped floors, they learned quickly that cleanliness was expected for a healthy environment. Since Ivy had no one to answer to, she could live as she pleased, and she did.

A normal weekday for Ivy consisted of managing a department store in the small town where she lived. In that environment, she was a very organized and tidy person. No one would have ever guessed at the disarray in her apartment. She made sure all of the sales counters were pleasant to look at, and the window displays were attractive. She managed the cleaning staff, and made sure the bathrooms were spotless at all times.   She loved how the bright lights overhead sparkled on the perfume bottles. The clothes on the mannequins always smelled of fresh fabric making her want to purchase a new outfit every other day, although she limited herself to one per paycheck. The discount helped to keep her closet full. Ivy was confused herself, by the fact that she could have such a sense of order at work. It was as if she only had so many hours a day in her of neatness, and then she exploded.   Dropping things off at her door, as she did, was her way of letting loose, shedding the tension, and forgetting all she had to deal with concerning her grandmother and her great-grandmother. She loved caring for and watching over them -- she wouldn't have it any other way -- but it could be trying at times.

Today had been an especially difficult day, seeing how her grandmother was going downhill. The disease was progressing quicker than they had predicted. A single tear rolled down Ivy's face. She dropped herself on the couch, and put her head on the pillow for few quiet moments of reflection. Slowly her eyelids closed and she began drifting off into a kinder place of grandma kisses and hugs. Suddenly there was a force of weight which landed on her stomach forcing her to expel air, and then a gentle purring followed.

"Percy! Could you find an easier way to make your entrance?" As the Siamese rubbed his head on her chin, pushing and banging, she laughed out loud. "Thanks, Percy, I needed that. You are such a good buddy. What would I do without you?"

"Meow"

"Oh, you're right. It's past time for dinner. Okay, let me get you something."

Percy jumped down with a gentle landing, barely making a sound as his paws made contact with the carpet, and then the excited cries for his meal pierced the air. Siamese had an innate ability to sound like a crying baby. It could be quite annoying at times, but when it turned into back and forth conversation, Ivy loved it. It was like having another person in the house with her, someone to share with, and someone to love. She placed the bowl of canned cat food on the floor;

Percy immediately began his gentle licking and lapping. The care he took eating his meal always made Ivy laugh. It was as if he were high society or royalty, having been taught exquisite manners. A lap here, a lick there. She loved how he closed his eyes as he savored the flavor of each morsel. Just watching him eased the tension of the day.

"Okay, Percy, now that you've had your meal, I have to think about mine. What should I have? Hmm? Left-over pizza? No, it's all gone. Oh, here's a part of a sub sandwich from yesterday's lunch. No, there's not enough there. What's in this bowl in the back?" Ivy lifted the cover and gagged – green mold and fluffy white stuff attached itself to whatever the contents had been at one time. She quickly put her hand over her mouth and walked the bowl to the garbage, dumping the remains. Then she filled the bowl with hot soapy water to soak. "Well, that ruined my appetite." She sighed. Eating alone was not fun. She hated going to a restaurant and ordering. The wait for the food with no one to talk to was awful. She usually had a book with her so her eyes wouldn't roam and get caught looking at the people at the other tables.

"Sorry, Percy, there's nothing in the cupboards, because I haven't been shopping in a long time. I guess I have no choice but to go out again. I can't bear to order another pizza. You'll be okay for a few minutes, right?" She scratched his head as he licked his paws clean, but he was totally oblivious to her and her dilemma. "Cats! You could at least pretend you cared." She sighed, grabbed her purse and headed back out.

The air was crisp and cool. Fall had finally arrived in Whitehall. Ivy loved her small town situated at the east end of White Lake. So many towns had allowed the shopping malls and box stores to disrupt their quaint way of living, but even though Whitehall had many of those same big chain stores, as well as fast-food restaurants, it still had kept its small town charm.

Maneuvering her car was a much simpler task than it would have been had she moved to Muskegon as she had originally planned. But the main goal had been to be near her grandmothers once they were both placed in the nursing home, and since she was alone and could go wherever she chose, it had given her the opportunity to run from a bad situation with an ex.

The grocery store was just a few minutes from her house, so she made a quick stop planning to buy only a sandwich from their deli, but she also remembered she needed to pick up some milk for her breakfast cereal. She wasn't much of a cook and had no desire to learn, although she truly enjoyed food when someone else prepared it. She walked quickly through the store, totally unaware of her swinging stride, but one man kept his eyes on her as she bent over to pull out the gallon from the cooler. She looked so familiar to him that he couldn't stop himself from watching her. He enjoyed the slight roundness of her behind and the way her light brown, wavy, hair fell forward like a waterfall over a dam. The sun-kissed blonde streaks brought forth images of the changing currents found in the raging waters at the base of the fall. Fox made a concerted effort to hide his interest as he mulled over the sour cream choices, but he couldn't stop his eyes from darting over to see if he could get a full-on glimpse of her face.

Unfortunately, once she had the milk in the cart, she turned in the opposite direction, and he only had a view of her swinging hips once again as she moved away from him. Something was pulling him toward her, and before he knew it, his feet were moving quickly as he pushed his own cart toward the checkout lane, even though he had not yet completed his shopping list. He quickly glanced up and down the lines filled with people and their full grocery carts, but she was not there. Realizing she must have gone to another aisle to shop, he quickly turned his cart toward the breads, but at that very moment she was already exiting the snack aisle and they had completely missed each other. The lines were short at the self-check lane, so Ivy was able to check out in record time and was soon on her way, while he was left roaming the store, in hopes of finding her.

Chapter Four

Choking down the last bite of the frozen dinner she had selected at the store, Ivy made a mental note to begin to learn to cook. There was no reason she hadn't other than a lack of interest, but surely survival must be a motivating factor. She could not continue eating like this if she were going to spend the rest of her days alone, and so it seemed she would since there were no male prospects in this small town, and at 35, she was nearing the spinster age of 40. 'Was spinster still a word, anymore?' she wondered, angrily. She threw the cardboard package into the trash and put her fork and glass in the dishwasher. At least with TV dinners, cleanup was easy, and with its disposal she felt like she had cleaned her kitchen, but as she looked around, she saw a coffee pot with the old used filter still in it, and an opened box of cookies with crumbs spilling on the counter from the torn package. She quickly took care of the crumbs, more from a fear of mice and roaches than from a sense of order and cleanliness.

Deciding she would lay out her clothes for the coming day, she opened her closet and saw one lonely outfit on a hanger. All other options were in her clothes hamper or on the floor. How had that happened, she wondered? Didn't she just do her laundry last Tuesday? Then counting on her fingers, she realized it must have been the Tuesday before. Ivy didn't normally have such a hectic and busy life, but if she was honest with herself she would have to admit that visiting the nursing homes and seeing the grandmothers three to four times a week was cutting into her social life as well as the daily chores that needed to be done. Just the other day, a friend from work had asked her to go to the movies, but she had already promised GG she would come to the evening bingo game with her. And last week her neighbor and friend, Nancy, kept bringing up a blind date she had in mind for her. Ivy and Nancy had been getting quite close lately, and she hated to turn her down because she didn't have many friends, but as she explained, blind dates were not her 'thing.' She was always afraid she would be let down. There weren't too many men out there who met Ivy's specifications. She was looking for a gentleman -- someone who would pull out her chair, open her car door, and bring her flowers – a man like the stars in the old black and white movies. But for right now, she was really looking forward to a nice relaxing soak.

Just as Ivy began to draw a bath, her cell phone rang. For a moment she almost let it go to voice mail. She had been looking forward to hot soapy water while reading a good book, but then she thought better of letting the phone go unanswered. She picked up just in time, noticing the call was from the home. Her heart lurched as she answered with a breathy 'hello.' She had never received a call at home from Red Pine before in the evening.

"Hello, this is Annie at Red Pine Home for the Aged. Is this Ivy Morton?"

"Yes. What's wrong? Is GG okay?"

"Ivy, it's not GG. She's fine. But I think you'd better come as quickly as you can. Your grandmother, Olivia, has slipped into a coma. I'm afraid she doesn't have much time."

"Oh, oh no. Yes – yes, I'll be right there. Thank you for calling."

With shaking fingers, Ivy called Nancy. "Hullo?" said Nancy with a yawn.

"Nance, it's me. Did I wake you?"

"Oh, yes, but that's okay. I just dozed off while watching Judge Judy, I guess. What's up?"

"I have to go back to the home. My grandmother is in a coma."

"Oh Ivy, I'm so sorry. What can I do for you?"

"I'm not sure how long I'll be gone, maybe through the night. If I'm not back in the morning, will you be able to feed Percy?"

"Sure, of course."

"You still have a key, right?"

"Yes, the one you gave to me in case of emergency. Don't worry about a thing, and stay in touch, okay? I'll be praying that all is well."

"Well, you know the situation. I'm afraid this is not going to be a happy ending."

Ivy held back the tears just long enough to finish the conversation, and then she took a few minutes to cry before going out the door. She would need to be strong for GG.

Ivy quickly parked at the front of the long, low building. She ran to the main entrance and hit the button for the automatic door which moved interminably slow. Then she pushed on the bottle filled with hand sanitizer solution for her hands and ran through the next set of double doors. Annie was waiting for her at the front check-in desk. One look in her eyes was all Ivy needed to know. She was too late.

"Annie? Annie? What happened?"

Annie took Ivy's hands in both her own and said soothingly, "She went quickly. That happens sometimes. Come, let's sit on the sofa."

The vestibule/waiting area was beautifully decorated with comfortable sofas and overstuffed chairs. Side tables were covered with up-to-date magazines, and pots were filled with ferns and palms. This area was meant to be a place of refuge for family members. On occasion a resident would push their wheelchair here where they could look out at the garden, so that they might have a break from the hallways which were filled with the sick and dying.

At this time of the day there was no one here but the two of them.

"Tell me, Annie. I'm ready for the news."

Annie began with the same soft voice she had used many times before when dealing with family members and death, but it never got any easier for her. "Your grandmother passed away shortly after I called you, so don't beat yourself up; there was no time. As you know, when she was first diagnosed, she signed a Living Will and asked that when her time came she not be resuscitated, and we followed those directions. I'm sorry, but that's what she wanted."

"Yes, she told me many times that she didn't want to live if machines were the only thing keeping her alive, and she was terrified of the time when she would no longer recognize her family."

Ivy heard a soft sobbing and when she realized it was her own voice, she inhaled deeply, trying to get herself under control. Then she was led down the hall to say one last goodbye to her beloved Nana. After a few moments with her grandmother's body, she went to the chapel to say a prayer; she asked God to give her strength for the coming days. Then she slowly raised herself up from the pew, and with a heavy heart, she went to see GG.

≈

GG was surprisingly calm. The staff had wheeled her into her daughter's room as quickly as they realized Olivia's state. GG had sat at her bedside holding her hand and praying, and then a miracle happened. For a few brief moments her daughter opened her eyes. She looked directly at GG and simply said "Mama," then she smiled sweetly and quietly took her last breath.

"I'm so sorry I wasn't here, GG. I had no idea, or I wouldn't have left to go home. I would never have left you alone."

"I know, sweetheart. Don't worry about me. I have faced a lot of death in my time. When you get to be 101, just about everyone you've ever known is gone. And although no mother wants to see her child leave this Earth before she does, Olivia was 84 and sick, so it was expected. And look at it from my perspective; it won't be long before I see her again. She'll be with the good Lord, and she'll be completely healed. We'll be able to relate as mother and daughter again."

"Oh, please, GG, don't talk like that. I just lost her; I can't lose you, too." Ivy dabbed at her eyes with her wadded up Kleenex.

"It will happen when it happens and I'm ready, but not for a while yet. I'm too stubborn to go right now. I won't leave you yet, child." Ivy hugged her great-grandmother, and as they gave each other solace, she was planning what had to be done next. The first thing was to call her father; it was proper and her duty as a daughter, but was not looking forward to it.

The phone call to her father went as expected. Ivy was not able to talk to him because he was in one of his meetings, so she had to convey the message to her step-mother, who was the same age as Ivy. Ivy had long ago suspected that his 'meetings' were just an excuse to avoid talking to his daughter. As far as she knew her step-brothers, who were now in their pre-teens, had never even met Nana. Ivy had learned to block the whole family out of her life, except when necessary. She had no desire to have any kind of a relationship with Tawny, whose name sounded as if she was a stripper, and for all Ivy knew maybe she had actually been one. She certainly looked the part with her California bleached blonde hair and her fake boobs. Ivy left a message with Tawny, almost forcing the details on her, as she hadn't seemed the least bit interested. She said she would have her father call back when he could. Ivy disconnected, glad the call was finally over. The details of the funeral would be left to her, so she could follow Nana's instructions without any interference. And there was wonderful Annie, who stepped right in and offered her the use of the chapel and the in-house chaplain.

From that point things went quite quickly. Nana was cremated and the date was set for a small memorial at the home. Ivy's father flew in by himself at the last minute. He awkwardly hugged her and GG, showing no signs of mourning the loss of his own mother. The people in the home and the staff were more caring. Ivy tried to connect with her father and reminisce, but he had shut down to her. He only seemed to want to talk about his other family. They all felt a relief when the day was over, and he could fly back to California. Ivy didn't care if he was ever in her life again. She cried for the loss of her grandmother, and felt compassion for her GG's loss and pain, but she felt nothing for her own father who had walked out on her to chase after a younger woman.

After dropping her father at the airport, Ivy slowly dragged herself into her apartment. Percy was there to greet her. Nancy had been doing a wonderful job of taking care of him. Shortly after she closed the door, the doorbell rang, and then she heard a call, "Ivy? Are you home?"

She opened the door and fell, sobbing, into her friend's arms. "Oh, Nance. I'm so sorry. I didn't mean to cry on you."

"Well, who else can you cry with if it's not me? It's just terrible that you have no family other than GG who you can share your grief with. Here, let's go sit down. I brought you a casserole so you don't have to cook tonight."

"That's so kind, Nancy. What would I have done without you these last few days? How can I ever repay you?"

"Don't worry about it. That's what friends are for. Now let's get you something to eat, and then you can rest. I hope you're taking a few more days off of work."

"No, I promised to go back after the funeral. I've been away too long already, and besides it'll be good for me. I need to keep busy. All I have left is GG now."

"And me, don't forget. I'll be there for whatever you need."

"Thank you, Nancy. You've become such a good friend."

The women ate their meal, sometimes in silence and sometimes chatting about work and other people they knew. They managed to stay off of any kind of depressing subject. Ivy shed a few tears when they hugged goodbye; then she cuddled Percy before falling into bed in an exhausted sleep.

Part Two —

Beginnings

Chapter Five

Work at the department store was routine, and that was just fine with Ivy. She didn't really want to think too much or the pain would return. Her boss, Mr. Garvey, had tried to convince her to stay home at least one more day, but she wouldn't even consider the suggestion. And besides, she said, other employees didn't get extra time off for a grandparent so why should she. But Ivy was distracted and knew she probably wasn't doing a great job today. She found herself watching the large clock on the wall, impatiently waiting for her shift to end. She intended to get right back to Red Pine to make sure GG was doing okay.

The hands of the clock finally aligned themselves in the perfect position, so Ivy felt comfortable leaving. She gathered her coat and purse, and lightly threw her new red scarf around her neck, not even bothering to tie it in a fashionable knot as she usually did. She distractedly waved goodbye to those who were still working and walked out into a cold, fierce wind. Winter was apparently coming early this year, bringing with it a biting blast. The smell of fresh snow was in the air. A strong gust ripped her scarf off her neck and carried it down the parking lot, rolling and twisting in a small whirlwind. It landed at the feet of a man who was in total shock at the sight of a ruby red scarf wrapping itself around his ankles. He bent over, trying to untangle it, as Ivy ran towards him.

"I'm so sorry. The wind caught me by surprise."

When Fox stood up to hand the knitted neck-wrap to the woman, he was shocked to see the person he had been following at the grocery store a week ago. He was sure of it, he would never forget that sun-streaked hair. Her face was flushed from the jog across the lot, but it gave her a charming glow. Her eyes were a yellow-green catching all shades of light, but he noticed they were also red-rimmed and filled with sadness and sorrow.

He could tell they were on the brink of spilling over. His heart instantly warmed to her. He longed to wrap the scarf around her neck, pull her toward his chest, and give her comfort.

Ivy found herself looking up into the kindest brown eyes she had ever seen. He was taller than she was, slender – of what she could see through his jacket – very handsome in a clean-cut way, and he was wearing a fedora similar to what the men wore in the 1950s and '60s. It was tipped at a jaunty angle, making him resemble Don Draper, a character in Mad Men – her favorite TV show. She had watched the reruns over and over again. He even wore the same style three-quarter coat. The dimple in his chin made her yearn to reach out and touch it. She was sure he must have this effect on all women, yet he seemed unaware of his charisma.

"Is this errant scarf yours?" When he smiled his whole face lit up. Ivy found it almost impossible to answer his question. She had never been tongue-tied in her life and yet here she stood, completely unable to make her mouth form any words.

Then finally a sound came out that sounded more like a sputter. "Uh, yes. Yes, it is. I bought it at the nursing home where my grandmothers – my grandmother lives. I'm so glad it didn't trip you."

As he handed it to her, they each grabbed it in a different spot, causing a tangle once again. As they tried to right the wrong, their hands became wrapped together. The warmth Ivy experienced when her flesh touched his was enough to make her knees weak. He studied her face; it was obvious he was feeling the sensual connection, too. For a few seconds neither one was able to withdraw their gaze.

"Sorry," he said laughing softly, gently pulling his hands away, not wanting to alarm her. "It seems your scarf has a mind of its own. I'm Fox, by the way. Fox Marzetti."

"And I'm Ivy Morton." They shook hands, and then laughed when they realized they had just untangled touching hands and had no need for a formal greeting.

"Well, I'd better get going," said Ivy awkwardly. "I'm going to visit my grandmother, and I have to get there before her dinner hour."

"I see, and what do *you* do for dinner? Do you eat with her?"

"Oh, no, she eats in the dining hall with the other senior residents. She's at Red Pine, and she has a table of women she sits with every day. She looks forward to their conversation."

"And – uh, is there someone you go home to and have a conversation and a meal with?"

"Only my cat, Percy." Ivy suddenly realized she was giving this stranger way too much information about herself. It probably wasn't wise.

"I have to run inside to grab a quick birthday gift for my teenage niece. Would you be willing to meet me later for dinner? I really hate to eat alone. It could be in a public place, at a restaurant of your choice." Fox held his breath waiting for her response. He'd never been so taken by a female before. He hoped he hadn't pushed too quickly. He was not in the habit of picking up women. He definitely did not have a 'line' prepared. And more than anything, he didn't want to give her the wrong impression of him.

Ivy stared at him for a second longer than she should have. She was trying to sort out her feelings. One moment she was grieving and all she could think about was her loss and pain and the next she was considering going on a date. Was it a date? Ivy heard Nancy say, 'you've got to put yourself out there, or you'll be alone for the rest of your life.' Ivy clearly saw, now, that a lonely life did not sound appealing at all.

"Okay," she said, as she exhaled slowly. "I'll need about an hour. The Beach House Diner on Adams Street?"

Fox's heart lurched and then quickly went back into rhythm. She had agreed! He grinned and said, "I'll see you there, Miss Ivy Morton." Then he dipped his head in a slight nod, and walked away. A few feet from her, she could hear him whistle a tune.

"My goodness," she said to herself. "What's come over me? I've never done anything like this in my life. I hope I don't live to regret it."

≈

"GG, how are you today?"

"I'm fine, child. It just seems strange not to go down the hall for my daily visit with Olivia. But I'll adjust to the new routine, as I have through all the happenings in my life."

"You're so strong, GG," said Ivy with a sigh. "I hope I have half your fortitude when I'm your age – and sooner would be fine, too."

"Well, I don't have any other choice. At my age the end could come at any moment. When you're young, you can't imagine dying – it's scary. But soon enough, you realize you don't have a choice. It will happen when it happens as it does to all of us. It's completely out of our hands; it all depends on when the good Lord is ready."

"I suppose you're right." Ivy paused for a moment to gather her thoughts. Something had been rolling around in her head for the last few days and she didn't quite know how to approach it. "GG, you've got me thinking. You know I've always wanted to be an author. I'm not cut out to be a store manager for the rest of my life. It's okay for now, and I like the people, but my passion has always been for writing."

"Yes, I remember how you used to write me letters when you were young. They were always so descriptive. And I read some of the short stories you wrote in high school. You do have a gift, Ivy Mae."

"Thank you, GG. That leads me to my next point. You have a wonderful story to tell, or so I'm told."

GG laughed and a little snort escaped. "It all depends on how you look at it. But it was romantic, if I do say so myself, and a little dangerous, too. I had quite a ride, yes I did."

"You would never talk about it to me. Why is that?" Ivy bit her lower lip, waiting for the answer. This could change everything for her.

GG looked at her with an intense gaze. "I was afraid for you. I didn't want you to get romantic ideas about my life and maybe want the same for yourself. I was protecting you."

"I can understand that. But, GG, I'm all grown up, and I don't need your protection, anymore. Would you consent to being interviewed? I'd love to get your history down for future generations, or maybe even write a book about you."

Now GG laughed right out loud. "Silly girl, there's not much to write about me. If anything, it's the people I surrounded myself with. Now they were the famous ones – or infamous, I should say. I called them The Unforgettables."

"That's what I'm talking about. You have a real story, and it's all true, isn't it. Could I hear it? Would you trust me?"

"I have to admit to being ashamed with the way my life was back when I was young, but it all changed after – well, it all changed." A sadness passed over Ruby's face, and for that Ivy was sorry that she brought on bad memories to her beloved great-grandmother. Then Ruby sat up straighter and said, "You know, I'm not going to be around for too much longer. Maybe it's time I told you the whole thing, so you don't romanticize it too much."

"Oh, GG, that would be wonderful! I mean about sharing your story, not about you dying. I won't hear of that. You'll be with me for a long time to come. I need you now. You're all I have."

Her GG patted her hand and offered up a radiant smile, knowing all too well that her time was limited. But she was okay with that, because there were a lot of people that she was anxious to see on the other side.

Chapter Six

Ivy stood in front of the mirror turning around and around in order to view her backside. She wondered why was doing that. It was the same size as it was yesterday. She was usually pretty secure with her body shape; she knew she looked good, because men's eyes often followed her. It was all thanks to genes – mostly GG's – because Ivy did not like to exercise, and she never worried about what she ate. But now for the first time since she was a teen, she was twirling and spinning to get the best angle shown in the reflecting glass.

After leaving GG, Ivy had come home to feed Percy before meeting him – Fox. At first the plan had been to simply feed her cat, run a brush through her long hair, maybe put it up in a clip and then dash off to the diner.

But suddenly that didn't seem good enough. She carefully applied new make-up, enhancing her golden streaked eyes, then she selected a white, cashmere, V-neck sweater to go with her new jeans. She threw her burnt orange pashmina scarf around her neck and tied it in the new way Nancy had shown her. And finally, she added her small gold hoop earrings. She was hoping for a casual but well-put-together look. And after a careful viewing of her reflection, she was sure she had achieved her goal.

A soft knock on her door interrupted her thoughts. It would be Nancy, of course. She was happy she had decided to come over. Ivy felt the need of another woman's opinion. For some reason she was nervous about meeting a new man for dinner. "Come in," she called.

"I'm so glad you haven't left, yet," said Nancy, walking in without preamble. "I thought you might want to use my new Coach bag. That cross-body you've been using will completely mess up your scarf. Look, it's called glove-tanned pebble. It's the perfect color to go with your scarf – which looks gorgeous on you, by the way."

"Hi, Nance. You're so thoughtful. I was just wondering if I should switch purses. But I'm running late as it is. Do you think I'm overdressed for a diner?"

"No, not at all. You know there are people in this town of all financial levels. You never know who will be there. Dump everything out on the table. I'll help. Only take what's necessary. Here, take your keys, wallet, lipstick, and here's some Kleenex. Oh, and don't forget your cell phone. Is it charged? Just in case you need to call me."

"Yes, mother," laughed Ivy.

"Seriously, Ivy, don't go anywhere with him. You don't have a clue who he is. Just a meal at the diner, and that's it. And walk yourself to the car when you're ready to leave. Make sure you park in front of the diner in the lighted area. If you have any problem at all, call me. I'll be right there. Matt is working tonight, so I can take off whenever I need to." Nancy's husband of one year was a Whitehall firefighter. She still had a lot of adjusting to do to his occupation, but she had learned a lot of safety tips he had taught her that she was constantly passing on to Ivy.

"Okay, okay. I'm all set. Don't worry. It's just a casual get-to-know-one-another meeting. Two people who need to eat. Don't worry. It's not a real date."

"What do you call it, then? A date comes in all forms, and this definitely qualifies as a date."

The two young women hugged as they went out the door. Although Ivy had tried to act like this dinner didn't matter, she was more nervous than she had let on. There was something about Fox; she just couldn't put her finger on it.

A parking spot was waiting for her just a few spaces down from the door. Ivy pulled in expertly leaving just the right amount of space on each side. As she got out of the car, she pulled her coat a little tighter to her body. The temperature had dropped quickly and the wind had picked up a little. It was coming off White Lake which always lent a dampness and chill to the air, but tonight the breeze also brought the smell of Lake Michigan, which was just at the end of the channel. Most likely, they were in for a good storm.

The windows of the diner steamed when the contrast of the inside and outside temperatures collided, enclosing the eating area in a foggy cocoon; the aromas of grilled hamburgers and French fries wafted out the door as a lone customer exited. The man stepped back and held the door open for Ivy; he smiled at her with an inviting look as she passed closely by him. It had been a while since she received that type of flirtation from a male. She couldn't help but smile back. Something strange was happening with her lately. Suddenly male attention was coming her way; had she unknowingly been inviting it?

"Do we know each other?" he asked.

"No, I don't think so. Sorry, I'm meeting a friend. Would you excuse me?" He gave a gentle shrug of the shoulders as if to say, 'oh well, I tried.'

The diner was busy and noisy. Sounds of dishes clinking and pans clanging came from the kitchen, muffling the conversations from the customers, but bits and pieces could still be heard over their laughter and the background music. It was a happy place; the spot where the locals came together for a quick bite. Ivy scanned over the heads of the patrons, and quickly found Fox in a booth along the back wall. He was reading the menu and had not noticed her come in. Whether he saw the movement out of the corner of his eye as she approached, or sensed she was there, Ivy wasn't sure, but he suddenly glanced up with a bright smile showing off the features of his handsome face. He looked different with his hat off, but it was a pleasant surprise. When he began to get up, Ivy slipped into the booth on the opposite side before he had a chance. She was afraid he might try to hug her or kiss her cheek as a way of greeting, and she wasn't ready for that yet.

"Hi, I wasn't sure you'd come. You look nice." He suddenly seemed shy.

"Thank you. Of course I would come. I never back down on my word, and I realized that I didn't have your number, so I couldn't call to cancel if I wanted to."

"Did you want to?" he asked softly.

Ivy looked down at her hands, trying to still her heart. She pretended to be busy with her gloves. "No," she said, raising her eyes to his. "I didn't want to."

"Good. Now, what's the house specialty?"

She laughed. "Burgers. I take it you're not from here? Everyone knows this place has the best in town."

"No, I'm not. I live on the other side of the state – in the thumb area – Bay City." He used his hand as a typical way for Michiganders to describe their location in the mitten state. Fox lowered his head as he looked over the menu, giving Ivy a chance to study him a little. He was clean shaven, possibly with a fresh haircut, or maybe he always kept his hair perfectly in place like that. She was surprised at how dark it was, since she had only seen him with his hat on. It was styled with a side part and then brushed back on the top and sides, with a small amount of styling gel to keep it in place. He could have stepped right out of a 1950s catalog, except she guessed he couldn't be much over forty, if that. Ivy immediately placed herself in an old TV sitcom scenario where her husband had come home from a long trip. He would wrap his arms around his wife's small waist, her full skirt poofing out as he kissed her soundly before carrying her up the stairs to their bedroom. She sighed.

Fox glanced up, wondering what he had done wrong. "How's the grilled chicken sandwich?"

"What? Oh, it's great. They use a wonderful homemade sauce." Embarrassed that she had been caught daydreaming over a man she barely knew, she began to ramble about the menu until the waitress came to take their orders.

"So, tell me about yourself, Ivy Morton."

His eyes exposed crinkle lines as he smiled; his teeth were straight and white. Could a man be any more perfect? "Ivy? Did you hear me?"

"Oh, yes, of course. Sorry. Well, I grew up here. I lived away for a while, but recently moved back. I was raised by my father and grandmother – my mother died when I was young."

"I detect some sadness with that statement, and I thought I saw some in your eyes earlier today when we met."

"Yes, well, my Nana died recently, and I'm still grieving, I guess." Not wanting to put a damper on the evening, she went on. "But I still have my GG, my great-grandmother, that is. She's in Red Pine, also."

"Oh? She must be getting on in years, then."

"Yes, she's one hundred and one, now. And a spitfire. If it wasn't for her wheelchair, she'd still be pretty active. She's wonderful. Now, what about you? If you live in the thumb, why are you here on the western side?"

"Well, I'm into real estate, you could say. I check out houses, and do appraisals for a real estate company, but they also contract me out."

Ivy was a little disappointed to hear that Fox didn't live nearby, but it was only a first date, after all. And things might not work out, anyway. "Where did you get the name of Fox?"

He laughed. She loved the sound of his voice; it had a soft warm timbre. She wondered if he could sing. "A question asked by many."

"I'm sorry, was I too forward?"

"Not at all. I'm actually named after my mother's maiden name. That, and they were a little bit of the hippy type. You know, living off the land -- self-preservation. They were surprised when I wanted to go another direction, but they put up with me." Another velvety-voiced chuckle escaped. "What do you do for a living, Ivy?"

"I'm a department store manager, but that is not what I dream about doing with my life. I just haven't made a good start on that yet."

"And what is that?" There was a pause in the conversation while the waitress delivered their food, all greasy goodness, hot off the grill. Fox took a bite of his chicken and closing his eyes, he moaned a little. Ivy blushed as she imagined that moan escaping his lips for another reason. "So what is your life's dream, then?" he continued.

"Well, it's always a little embarrassing to say out loud, but I want to be an author."

"Why is that embarrassing?"

"You know, people think you're crazy. Only a few make it, and they say it's a pipe dream. But recently I've been inspired to go for it."

"What inspired you?"

"When my Nana died, it really sank in, then, that everyone has an ending, but we never know when that is. My mother died when she was 33; my grandmother made it to 84, and my great-grandmother is still living. There's no timetable. My GG has a great story, so she tells me, and I want to get her beginning down on paper before it's too late. I'm not sure what I'll do with it, but at least I'm going to start taking notes. I'll worry about the rest later."

"It sounds like a huge goal, but I'm sure you can do it." He loved watching her lick her lips as she ate. He found himself imagining what those lips could do to a man. Fox lightly cleared his throat, reminding himself not to get too far ahead.

"You know, I have something to confess. I've seen you before."

"You have? Where?" Ivy was startled. Should she have recognized him? She was positive they had never met, and yet –

"Well, I saw you the other day in the grocery store. But that wasn't really the first time I saw you. I thought you looked familiar then. And in the parking lot, when you mentioned your grandmother at Red Pine, I put it all together, but you seemed upset, and I didn't want to take it further. You see, I'm often in various nursing homes. I sometimes deal with properties owned by the elderly."

"Oh, I see, I think."

"Yes, well, I've seen you there. I was coming out of the office one day and you were pushing a woman in a wheelchair. You greeted everyone you passed and made them seem special. You're good with the elderly."

"Thank you. It's just that between the two grandmothers, I've been in that home for years. I know them all. It's hard to watch them pass away one by one. But it's a fact of life, and that's why I need to get GG's story down now."

"You certainly have the passion for it." At the word of passion, his eyes roamed over her face, taking in every detail. Her soft creamy complexion, full lips, the small tipped-up nose which gave her a childlike look, and eyes a man could get lost in.

As she had at their parking lot meeting, Ivy found herself staring back into this man's eyes; their color and depth were taking her to straight to his soul. She was getting attached too quickly; she was afraid of losing her head. She changed the subject away from herself, and they continued on for a while with light chit chat.

A quick glance at the clock told her it was getting late. Ivy took a sip of her pop and said, "I – I, uh, think

I'd better get going. There might be a storm coming in. I don't have far to go, but I'd rather not get caught in it."

"I understand. Can I have your cell number, for the next time I'm in town?"

"Yes, of course. What's yours? I'll text it."

After exchanging numbers, he paid the bill and never even questioned whether it should be split. A true gentleman. He walked her to her car, and even though Ivy heard Nancy's warning voice in her head, she wasn't worried that she had let him. They hugged goodbye. Ivy almost melted into his arms when she smelled his after shave – Old Spice. Of course, she thought. As she backed her car out of the space, he waited to watch her drive away. When she waved, he tipped his hat. Had she finally found the man of her dreams? She wondered if she would ever hear from him again.

Chapter Seven

The lounge at Red Pine was busy today. Ivy had pushed GG into the entrance of the room, but as they looked around they could not find one chair available for Ivy's use. And the other downfall was that the TV was always on a loud setting so the residents with hearing disabilities could hear, although Ivy always wondered why the set was on in the first place. It was usually set to a sports or game channel. Most of the geriatric patients had been pushed in here by an aide, even though they each had a TV in their own rooms. She supposed it was for stimulation and a sense of being around other people. Some slept through their whole afternoon.

"Well, GG, this is not going to be good for our purposes. It's crowded and it's too loud."

"We can't stay in my room," snorted GG. "That old biddy in the bed next to me will repeat everything I say to you."

"GG! That's not like you."

"Well, she's just become such a busybody. I have to be careful all the time or she blabs to Esther, and before you know it, my news gets around the whole place!"

"Okay, well I can understand that you'll want privacy. Let me see what I can do. Can I leave you here for a minute?"

"Sure, just don't be too long. I'm not a soccer fan."

Ivy hustled off to the nurses' station. She hoped they wouldn't make her wait; she had limited time with GG today, and she was anxious to get started. As luck would have it, a young woman was sitting at the desk and for a change did not have the phone to her ear.

"Can I help you?"

"Yes, I'm with Ruby Hanson. I was wondering if there's a quiet room we can use. I'm taking down her life story so I can write a book about her someday, and we need some privacy."

"Wow, isn't that interesting. I can imagine that she has led quite a fascinating life. I've always been interested in the back stories of our residents, and someone who has lived as long as she has must have a lot to say." She smiled kindly at Ivy. "I don't believe we've met. I'm kind of new here. My name is Jill. I'm assigned to Ruby's hall."

"Nice to meet you, Jill. My name is Ivy Morton. I'm GG's – uh, Ruby's great-granddaughter."

"I'll tell you what. The conference room is open right now. You can use the table, and the chairs there will be more comfortable, too. If it works out, we can schedule an hour or so a week for your usage. We just have to put it on the calendar."

"Oh, that would be perfect. Thank you so much."

"It's just down the hall and to the left. You can't miss it."

"Thank you, so much, Jill."

"Just get me a copy of that book when you finish." She winked at Ivy as she walked away.

≈

Ivy pushed Ruby up to the long table and seated herself on the opposite side. She laid out her tablet and pens, and then next to that, she placed her new digital recorder. "This is what I'm going to record your voice on, just in case I get my facts wrong on paper."

"Oh, I don't know about recording my voice. You didn't say anything about that."

"It's nothing scary, GG. We just talk like normal, and then I can listen to it later when I'm at home. Just regular conversation. Can we give it a try?"

"Okay, as long as I don't have to be perfect. I might misremember a few things and have to back up now and then."

Ivy laughed. "I highly doubt that! You have the best memory of anyone I've ever known."

"Okay, then, where do you want to start?"

"Go back as far as you can remember, when you were a child. Tell me what life was like then."

"Well, let's see. I was born in 1915. Of course, I don't remember anything for a few years. I had a younger brother named Henry who died of The Spanish Flu, or the influenza as we called it then. I do remember that. That was a terrible time. I learned later, when I was older, that the flu ran rampant all over the world from 1918 to 1920. A real pandemic, you would call it today. I guess I got sick, too, but somehow I survived. It was especially deadly for children. My mother was afflicted with it, also. She was the first one of the family to fall ill, and after she recovered Henry got sick. She always felt that she had passed it on to him and it was her fault that he died, but he probably would have gotten it anyway, as I did. Mother was never the same after that. She was weak and was bedridden most of the time. By the time I was seven, she had passed away from tuberculosis, which was another terrible disease in the early 1900s. She spent the last years of her life in a sanatorium, so I really don't have much of a memory of having a mother.

"My father, Earl Shaeffer, did the best he could, but he was busy. By the early '20s, he had added a gas station to his auto repair garage. – Shaeffer's Auto, it was called. The gas pumps were in front of our house. We lived right on U.S. 131 – of course it didn't look anything like it does now. There was no such thing as an expressway, then. It was just a dusty road. The auto repair shop was in a separate building next to the house. We had the only gas station for miles. Since automobile travel was still fairly new, it was highly needed in those parts. People would stop to fill up their cars and trucks and also fill an extra gas can or two just in case they ran out before the next station. To this day the smell of gasoline brings back memories." Ruby stopped to smile to herself. Ivy thought she saw tears and a frown fill her eyes, also.

"Are you doing, okay, GG?"

"Sure, I can go on for a bit longer, but then I have to get to Bingo. Are we still recording? Okay, let's see, where was I?"

≈

Ruby's story went on for weeks, recorded a little at a time, sometimes with joy, sometime with tears, but Ruby plugged away, even when her voice was weak. She was now eager to release the story that she had been keeping from her great-granddaughter and all the others in the family, spilling it so quickly that Ivy had trouble taking notes. At times, Ivy could tell that Ruby felt like she was actually living those moments all over again. Now glad she had purchased the recorder, she prayed there wouldn't be a mechanical failure.

They talked through the fall and into the winter, one hour at a time. Ivy would go home and download the day's recordings to her computer. She would listen to everything all over again and make notes and questions for the next day's session. But soon the day came when GG's heart began to grow weak. She told Ivy she knew she didn't have much time left, but she wanted to make sure that Ivy inherited her house at Wabaningo on White Lake and all of her belongings, so she adjusted her will, which now excluded Ivy's father and his other off-spring.

Just after GG finished telling her story, she began to grow weaker. It was as if she knew she had said everything she wanted to, and it was okay to go. When Ivy received a call in the early morning hours, just as she had when her Nana died, it wasn't a shock, but she was stunned just the same. Ruby had passed away quietly in her sleep, at the age of 102, with a smile on her face -- and that's when Ivy's world came to an end.

For days and weeks Ivy followed a boring routine. She went to work and came home. She wasn't interested in anything else. Her father had not come home for the funeral, using the excuse that he was out of the country working on a big deal. Ivy was through with her father. She had been hurt too many times; she didn't care if she ever saw him again. The service was held right at the home with all the residents and nurses in attendance; Ivy was pleased that so many people loved Ruby.

She had received several texts from Fox, but since he didn't know about GG, the words were upbeat. 'Can we meet? I'll be in West Michigan next week.' Or, 'I haven't heard from you. Hope all is well.' She didn't respond. Talking about her loss was too much for her to handle. Even Nancy had to tiptoe around the subject. She worried about Ivy and tried to mother her, but nothing seemed to work.

One day in the early spring, when hope of new life was just around the corner, Nancy dared to approach the idea of the book Ivy had wanted to write.

"Maybe by going over your notes, you'll feel closer to your GG. It's not right to ignore all of the work you two did together."

Ivy stared at her for a long time, almost unable to answer, and then a light seemed to go on. "You're right

– my notes and recordings. I'd forgotten all about those."

"Maybe it would be like honoring Ruby, if you could put it all down for others to read."

"I'm not sure if I want others to read it or not, but it would give me a project to work on that involved her. Thank you, Nancy. I think it's just what I need. I'm going to start my book!"

Nancy breathed a sigh of relief. Ivy was going to be all right. She was coming out of her foggy haze. She hugged her friend and said, "Take it slow, take all the time you need. It'll be good for you."

After going over her notes and making an outline, Ivy began the long process of creating a book. She spent all of her free time writing; sometimes her thoughts were flying so fast that her fingers could barely keep up, and other times, she would stop and sob at the remembrance of her good-natured great-grandmother, especially now knowing the kind of life she had had. When she had finished writing and editing the final chapter, she reread the whole thing beginning to end, and when she turned the last page, she knew what she had to do. It was exactly what Ruby would have wanted.

once when she turned the lamp pose. The lamp went out. She had to . . ." was more to which Celeste told Ira wanted.

Part Three –

Ruby's Story

Chapter Eight

After her mother died, Ruby had a tough time. She was only seven years old, with no knowledge of how to run a household. Her mother had spent time showing her how to wash dishes and sweep a floor; she was even taught how to use a knife and cut some vegetables, but other than that she was clueless. For a while some of the ladies in the community would stop by to help. They taught her how to do laundry and how to make soup and a few other easy dishes, and they showed her how to do simple mending. They would quite often bring some food for supper along with them. One woman, in particular, would linger long enough for Ivy's father, Earl, to finish with work, as far as the repair shop was concerned, and in order to show his gratitude, he would invite the lady to stay and eat with them. It soon became apparent that she was looking for a husband. Her father wasn't ready for another spouse yet, even though he knew it would be best for Ruby. 'She's doing just fine,' he said. 'She's learnin' real quick, and we're gettin' along.'

Ruby struggled to do the household chores, while going to school. As she got older her father added more responsibilities to her day. At the age of nine, she was getting up before light to make breakfast for her Pa and to get herself ready for the long walk to school. School was the only place where she was allowed to be a kid. She especially loved recess when the girls would stand in huddles and gossip and the boys would play kick the can. One day Jimmy Beck chased her and kissed her on the cheek. It was the first kiss she could ever remember getting, other than from her Ma when she was sick in bed and would ask for a kiss goodnight. Pa was not affectionate at all. For him, it was all about fixing cars and pumping gas. He was always worried about money and where they would get their next meal. Life at home was not happy for the little girl.

As cars began to frequent the roads more, and life in the country revolved around keeping a farmer's Model A pickup truck running, her Pa became more and more engrossed in his work. The bell would ring at all hours when a customer needed gas, and Pa would have to get out of bed, pull up his pants and suspenders, and go out to help a motorist in need. Ruby wondered why people where driving so late at night. But as the bell rang more often, it seemed that Pa had a little more money, so she never complained. One day he bought her a new ribbon for her hair. She wore it to school proudly, no longer feeling less than the other girls. But shoes and dresses were still a problem. Mrs. Corker, down the street, had made it her mission to bring Ruby hand-me-downs from her older daughter, and although Ruby appreciated the gesture, the dresses never fit just right since Mrs. Corker's daughter was quite a bit overweight and Ruby was as skinny as a rail.

Eventually, Ruby learned to be a better cook, and actually began to bake. She was really good at doing laundry, and on nice days she enjoyed hanging the clothes on the line. On rainy days they would have to string the clothing up on ropes inside the house, so they could dry by the stove. Luckily, neither one of them had much to wear, so it didn't take up too much space, but her pa would have to duck his head to get from the kitchen to the living room.

Getting to school was still a struggle, especially in the winter, but the law required Ruby to attend until she was fourteen or had graduated eighth grade. Sometimes if Pa was repairing someone's vehicle and he needed to 'test drive' it, he would give her a ride. He only did that, though, on the cars that belonged to the locals. If one of the men in the big black cars dropped off a vehicle, he never drove it at all, other than to take it down the road and back for a half mile. Sometimes the men would wait on the front porch of the house for their vehicles. They would play cards or checkers at the table Pa had set up for them. Ruby got quite an education with the language that was freely floating around. On hot days Ruby was expected to supply them with drinks – cold water, lemonade, or liquor which was always present, even though it was illegal. Ruby never knew where it came from, but suddenly there would be a few bottles in the cupboard.

In 1916, just one year after Ruby was born, the State of Michigan adopted the Damon Act and it was enforced as of 1917, three years ahead of the National ban. Everyone around knew what the Damon Act was. It made buying, selling, and drinking alcohol of any kind illegal in all counties. In other words, Michigan was dry – and yet, liquor was in their kitchen cupboard. In 1919 Michigan joined other states to ratify the 18th Amendment to the Constitution, making the sales and use of alcohol illegal all over the United States. So by 1920 the Prohibition era was in full swing. Ruby never told anyone about the men or the bottles. She wondered what would become of her if her Pa went to jail. And even though most of the men were respectful, she was terrified of them. Once in a while, one of them looked at her in a strange way or made a comment that caused all of the others to laugh. She wasn't sure what the words meant, but she knew whatever they had said wasn't proper.

One day, when she had reached the age of thirteen, she complained to her father about what one of the men had said to her. She repeated the words exactly as they were said, though she really didn't understand them. Even with all of the salty language she had heard while growing up, these words had never been spoken in her presence before. She was shocked when her father slapped her face. "Never say those words out loud again to anyone. You hear?" he yelled. Then he shook her hard by the shoulders. The red bruise was still visible on her cheek the next day, so she couldn't go to school. After that, she made sure she was out of sight whenever one of those cars pulled up. She found other tasks to do by weeding the vegetable garden, or working on the mending in her room.

The day finally came when she had completed the eighth grade. For Ruby, school had been the only escape from the drudgery at home, and even though she wasn't the best student, she still enjoyed learning and being around the other girls and boys. Then at the end of the summer, when she asked her Pa about a new dress for school, he looked at her in surprise.

"What are you talking about?"

"School, Pa. I need a new dress. My old one is worn, and besides, it's too small."

"But you graduated. There's no more school for you."

"Pa, I'm allowed to go all the way to high school. I don't have to quit after the eighth grade."

"I'm afraid you do, Ruby. I need you here. It's been hard enough all these years letting you go off all day while I struggled to run the business by myself."

Ruby was shocked. All of her friends were continuing on. She had assumed she would, too. For the first time she felt defiance building, and she knew it was about to boil over. She looked her father in the eye and calmly said, "Maybe it's time you got a wife instead of those floozies you see in town, and stop using your child as a slave to keep your house."

He had hit her before, but never like this. A slap to the face was sure to cause a black eye; a punch to the head made her see stars; and then he pushed her to the floor and kicked her in the stomach. His face turned a deep shade of red when he realized what he had done, and then he stomped out of the house. The next time she saw her father he was so drunk he could barely stand. She led him to his bed and took care of him like a good daughter should.

In his drunken stupor, she heard him mumble, "I should never have let them come around, Ruby, but I needed the money. And how was I to stop it, anyway?" There were no words of apology other than that before he passed out. Things were never the same between them after that.

Chapter Nine

The summer of 1929 was unseasonably warm, and the same balmy weather pattern carried through the fall. As the days came and went, slowly rolling one into another, Ruby often found herself wondering about her future and what her life would be like. Was she doomed to stay with her Pa forever, suffering his abuse and neglect? Contact with other children her age was limited to an occasional trip to town with her father when they needed dry goods, and food staples like flour, salt, and sugar. When she saw one of her old friends, she was embarrassed at how she looked and so she mainly kept her eyes lowered, until one of the girls would say hello. She would study their new hairstyles, and try to memorize the way they tied their bows and ribbons. Then when her father was not around she would fashion her hair in the newest look, but she would quickly pull the pins out when she heard him coming in. Short hair worn close to the head was the fashion for adult women, but Ruby knew her father would never allow her to cut her hair. She dreamed every day, now, of leaving this place, but how and when she could accomplish her departure, she didn't have a clue.

Winter came with a fury, as if to say, okay you've had enough warm weather for a while – now it's time I show what I can really do. The snow was deep and the wind was fierce for much of the season, causing drifts that were tough to navigate. Ruby was pretty much house bound, except for an occasional time when she would have to grab her coat and pull on boots that were too small for her to run outside and pump someone's gas. The roads were difficult to navigate so travel was limited for most people, except for the large black cars that kept arriving during the night. Her father was drunk more often than not when he wasn't working on a car. He no longer bothered to bathe and the stubble on his neck was becoming a full beard. He wore the same bib-top blue jeans day in and day out. They were grease-stained from his habit of wiping his hands on his pants, and they smelled of oil, gas, and sweat. Ruby washed as often as she could and brushed her hair the first thing every morning, but throughout the day her long, sandy brown curls would get tangled and matted, and with no mirrors in the house she had no idea how disarrayed she looked.

In June of 1930, Ruby turned fifteen. Her father never even acknowledge her special day, but that was no different than it had been in the past. Ruby did not remember ever getting a birthday or Christmas gift in her life from her father. Then, without preamble, on that same day she became a woman. In that era, she was right on schedule for how her body was maturing. She had heard the girls talking about their time of the month last year in school, so she had known a little of what to expect, but now that her time was here, she wasn't really sure what to do about it. She pretended to be sick and stayed in her room all day long, except to

107

come out to make her father his meals. Luckily, she was able to find some clean rags that were not soaked in oil and grease, so she fashioned what she needed with those. Then the next time she went to town with him, she managed to corner the store owner's wife. Embarrassed as she was, she had no choice but to ask how to deal with her monthly situation. The kind woman gave her a quick lesson on how to care for herself. She patted her on the back, muttering 'poor child,' and told Ruby if she ever needed anything, she would be glad to help.

Ruby dipped her head in shame, and quietly said, "Thank you, Mrs." and then her father yelled at her to hurry up, saying he needed to get back to his pumps.

From that day on Ruby began to see changes in her body. A fullness appeared on her chest, and her old dress began to strain against it. She was no longer a gangly twelve-year-old, but on the verge of becoming a full-grown woman. She was still slim-hipped, but there was a roundness to her bottom that hadn't been there before. Whenever she had to help a customer, she noticed the men looking at her in a new way. She could feel their eyes follow her as she walked away from them; a few times there were cat calls and whistles. She always ignored anything they said to her, afraid of her father's wrath.

Day in and day out Ruby did her father's bidding. Washing, cleaning, cooking was her way of life. There were no dances, parties, or gatherings of any kind. She was alone in a sea of motor vehicles that came and went endlessly like the waves of the tide. During that time, she grew taller and developed a natural grace. She would dream of a day when she could leave here; maybe she could be one of those beautiful women she saw on the magazine covers in town. Maybe she could marry a prince and have other people wait on her all day long for a change. She would ring a bell for her tea, and ask for sweets any time of the day. Someone would twist her hair up in the latest fashion before she went to a holiday ball. On those occasions, when she was daydreaming, Ruby often found herself humming a little tune as she imagined herself swirling around the dance floor with a handsome man. But there were no handsome men to her liking anywhere around, so she soon had to face the fact that she would have to find a way out on her own.

One day in August, on a scorching hot day, Ruby was hanging clothes out to dry. She hummed a little tune as she worked, happy to be outside in the fresh air. She had twisted her hair up in a bun, but the breeze moved short wisps about her face. Her dress was damp in the front from holding the wet clothes to her body as she fought the occasional gusts of wind. The fabric had molded itself to her form. Her dress was shorter than it should have been for the time period. Even though the modern women of the day had hiked up their hemlines, it was not appropriate for the young girls to do so. She was stretching to reach the clothesline when a gust came up and blew her skirt even higher exposing her well-shaped calves and a hint of thigh. It was then that she heard a low wolf whistle. Ruby turned around quickly and found herself looking at the most handsome man she had ever laid eyes on.

"Well, well, well. What do we have here?" He was tall and lean and extremely well-dressed, for this area which had been so badly affected by The Great Depression. He wore a white shirt, open at the collar; his sleeves were rolled up to the elbow. His high-waisted pants were held up by suspenders, and his jacket was slung casually over his shoulder. His newsboy hat sat at a crooked angle, and he sported a cocky grin to go with it. He was young but still a man; it was the first time that Ruby's heart had skipped a beat when looking at a male; she felt the tug of an unfamiliar yearning.

"Who - who are you and why are you in my back yard?" She noticed he was staring at her dampened chest, and instead of the revulsion she usually felt when one of her father's customers did the same thing, this time she felt weak in the knees and breathless. She took a step backwards, almost falling over the laundry basket, then slowly covered her bodice with the towel she had in her hands. He smiled when he saw her delay in doing so; he took it as an invitation.

"Oh, sorry, miss. I was just looking for the outhouse."

"It's on the other side of the garage – the one for customers, that is."

He ducked his head with an acknowledgement of thanks, but as he turned to go, he tipped his hat and said, "By the way, my name's Salvatore D'Angelo, but you can call me Sal." Ruby picked up on an Italian accent with a tinge of Chicago thrown in. He waited for her to respond with her name, but when none was forthcoming, he nodded again and left her standing there with a heart that was beating so hard she thought it might come out of her chest.

Ruby wasn't sure what had happened to her when she first saw Salvatore, but it didn't stop her from thinking about him. She dreamed about him every night. Whenever a car pulled up and honked their horn for service, she would run to the window to see if he was in it. Since she had been in the back yard the first time she laid eyes on him, she had no idea what kind of car he had arrived in. When she questioned her father as

112

to whether any new cars had come in for repair that day, he replied with his usual scowl, saying, "What business is it of yours?"

Her thoughts of Salvatore became an obsession. She imagined every scenario she could think of as to how their next meeting would go. She had many sleepless nights thinking that he might be in one of the many cars that passed through in the middle of the night, and she had probably missed him.

Then one day late in October, while Ruby's father was in the garage, she decided to sneak in a little break. She sat in the rocking chair on the porch and prayed for the return of Salvatore. She asked God to give her one more glimpse of him, so she could refresh her memory of his face. But no one came, and as she stood to go back into the house to continue with her daily chores, she lingered a moment, leaning against the post, taking in the fresh air. It was then that she heard a motorcar coming down the road. Usually, that was her cue to go inside, not wanting her father to yell at her to pump the gas, but they didn't all stop, and she was hesitant to start working again, so she remained.

A large 1928 Cadillac, with a green body and black roof and fenders pulled up at the pump. Ruby found her feet frozen to the spot when Salvatore emerged from the driver's seat, came around the car, and opened the door for his passengers. Salvatore was in a suit, vest, and tie, and this time he wore a homburg hat sitting properly on his head, at just a slight angle. Ruby couldn't believe the man of her dreams had finally appeared.

Three men got out of the car, but it was the man who last exited who immediately drew her attention. He wore a long coat, even though it was warm out, and he, too, wore a black homburg on his head. He had white spats snapped over his shoes and when he turned to look at her, she noticed three deep scars running down his cheek. Having seen posters in the post office for the FBI's most dangerous criminal list, she was shocked when she realized that the famous Al Capone, also known as Scarface, was standing in front of her.

Ruby wanted to run inside, but if she did, she would miss speaking with Salvatore.

Salvatore's boss said something to him, and as he gestured toward Ruby, he chuckled the way all men did when they looked at her now. Ruby could see Salvatore's face color, he nodded, and then he walked directly toward her. When he approached the porch, he tipped his hat, and said, "Good afternoon, miss. I'm Salvatore D'Angelo. I believe we met a while back, but I never got your name."

"I'm – my name is Ruby. Ruby Shaeffer. My Pa owns this place."

He smiled that flirtatious way he had, with his white teeth and teasing eyes; it seemed to Ruby that the birds were singing just for her. "I see. Well, my boss over there needs to have a meeting with your father, but first he would like to know if he can have some water."

"Sure, of course. I'll get a pitcher and bring it right out." Ruby knew by the heat she felt rising on her face that she was blushing, but she managed to give him a small smile in return. It was then that her father came out of the garage. He quickly walked over and invited Mr. Capone to sit on the porch. Ivy excused herself, and went inside for some cold water. When she returned the men were seated at the table, and as she poured the water, she was aware of Mr. Capone's eyes following her. He chuckled, and said, "Ya gonna let this one get away, Salvatore? Go on. We don't need ya here."

"Yes, sir. I won't be long."

"I'm sure you won't." The men laughed raucously, and Ruby was surprised and humiliated to see her father join in.

Chapter Ten

By the time Salvatore had followed her in, Ruby had moved to the sink to begin scrubbing a pan. She was afraid to look at him, embarrassed by the way she had been treated by the men, ashamed that her father had not defended her.

The man of her dreams moved slowly toward the kitchen counter; Ruby could barely breathe. Excitement and fear gripped her, holding her in a frozen pose. Salvatore stood next to her and then slowly turned so he was resting his backside near the sink. They were face-to-face, eye to eye. Ruby could see the slight stubble growing from his pores; a dark curl escaped his hat and rested on his forehead; his chocolate eyes were intensely focused on hers.

"How old are you, Ruby?" he asked softly. His voice was barely a whisper; she would not have been able to hear him had they not been so close.

Ruby was almost afraid to answer. Should she tell him the correct age and risk looking like a child in his eyes, or should she lie and add another year to make her appear more of a woman? Maybe the correct approach was to pretend she was younger, so he would be turned off by her youth and leave. Even though she was terrified, she was drawn to him like a moth to a flame. One thing she did know was that after all of her dreams of seeing him again, she did not want him to leave, so she decided to take her chances.

Ruby lifted her chin in rebellion and said, "I'm seventeen."

Salvatore tilted his head back and laughed. "You, Miss Ruby, are not seventeen. Did you add an extra year on for my benefit?" He reached out and touched her lightly on the cheek.

Ruby pulled her head back a little, but not before she allowed a slight caress to trail her jawline. Then, remembering her promise to herself to find a way out, she smiled flirtatiously, and said, "You're right, I'm actually sixteen, Mr. D'Angelo."

"Of course, you are." He chuckled, guessing that she was still not being truthful. "You're an adorable thing, and a real beauty, you know that? Has anyone ever told you that before? You're the kind of girl a man would want to keep forever. I know a lot of girls are already getting married at your age, but don't rush it. There's something special about you, Ruby Shaeffer. I'll be back this way again, driving for Mr. – uh, the guys, I mean, and every time I come you'll be a little older." He paused and then whispered in her ear, "Wait for me." And with that, he wrapped one arm around her waist and pulled her in closely to him. It was Ruby's first experience with a real kiss; his lips on hers felt different than she had expected – soft and warm. It was like sitting around a cozy fire with a blanket wrapped around her, while at the same time having a cool breeze caress her nakedness. Looking at her intensely, he asked softly, "Was that your first kiss, Ruby?"

She nodded weakly, unable to speak. The color had risen to her cheeks. She held her breath, afraid he would laugh at her. Instead he stared at her a long time, and then said once again, "Wait for me; okay, doll? And call me Sal."

When he slowly released her and walked away, Ruby almost passed out. She had just lied to a man with a shady character. She knew nothing about him other than he drove the car of a very famous person who was wanted by the law, and she was more frightened than she had ever been. But at the same time, she was also weak in the knees with his closeness, and the kiss which could have been rough and brutal if had he chosen it to be that way. And there would have been no one to protect her; her father seemed more than willing to give her up to him. But instead when their lips first met, it had been soft and tender and fitting for a girl her age completely lacking in experience.

When the screen door slammed, she could hear the men burst out in laughter. One said, "We knew you wouldn't keep us waiting. I would have thought your youth would give you more stamina." A chair squeaked and he said, "Well, I guess I'm next."

Ruby came out of her daze in an instant. She was on the verge of dashing out the back door, when she heard Sal say firmly, "No, she's mine. Leave her alone." And then, "What gives you the right?" Next, she heard the sound of fists hitting flesh and body. A chair broke as two men tumbled to the porch floor. A gunshot rang out, apparently into the air, as no one yelled out at the pain of injury.

Then Mr. Capone said firmly, "Benny, let Sal have her. He deserves her; he's earned it. Now, get up and let's get out of here. Clean yourself off, both of you! I have business to take care of."

When Ruby was able to move, she ran out the back door, afraid someone would change their mind. She heard voices, but was unable to detect any words from that distance, and then she watched as the large heavy car was driven down the highway by Salvatore D'Angelo, or Sal as she would always think of him from that day on.

When she returned to the house to finish the dishes, her father was standing there with disgust in his eyes, assuming the worst of her. Without saying a word, he slapped her hard on the face, then went back to his work in the garage.

Chapter Eleven

Things changed for Ruby throughout that fall and winter. Even though she was still a child, she had now lost all innocence about her father's business. She wondered how it was possible that she had not known that her own Pa was in cahoots with gangsters. As each vehicle pulled up in the middle of the night, she would sneak out of bed and peak out of the front window to see if Sal was one of the men whose voices she heard. Sometimes she was brave enough to open the door a crack to get a better view. It was on one of these nights that she saw a truck being unloaded with boxes that were then carried into the garage. The following night another truck, with a Patterson Dairy sign painted on the side, loaded up those very same boxes and then drove off into the dark night. From what she could see, Sal was never with them.

One evening right before Christmas, on a cold clear night, a car parked in front of the gas pump. Ruby heard the crunch of boots on the newly fallen snow. Earl had gone out to attend to the customer, and then two men followed her father to the garage. There was a light tap on the door. Now fully aware of what kind of people they had been dealing with, Ruby froze in fear. But then she heard a voice call softly, "Ruby, are you in there? It's me, Sal."

She dropped her stirring spoon and whipped the apron over her head, then smoothed her hair as best she could. Trying to act as casual as possible, she opened the door for him. He stepped inside, and placed his cool lips on hers, tasting her warmth and transferring it to himself.

"Ruby, I've been wanting to see you for so long, but this is the first time I've driven this way from Chicago." Then he stepped back to look at her, his eyes caressing her entire body as he took in her youthfulness, which was on the verge of the womanly beauty he knew would come in another year or two.

Ruby could not contain herself any longer. She let out a little squeal of happiness and then wrapped her arms around his neck and kissed him back with a passion she wasn't aware that she had in her. She pushed her body up against his, then rested her head on his shoulder for a moment. For the first time in her life, Ruby felt like she was truly where she belonged; her loneliness had disappeared.

Sal pulled back a moment, and laughed, saying, "Doll face, have you been practicing on someone else?"

Ruby blushed, lowered her head in embarrassment, and then raised her eyes to meet his. "I'm just happy to see you. I've been waiting for you to come back, just like you said."

Sal chuckled and pulled her back in, "Ruby, you're just precious. Look what I brought you. I've only got a second, but I wanted to give you a Christmas present. I thought a girl like you would appreciate it."

Ruby wasn't quite sure what a 'girl like you' meant, but she eagerly took the package from him and opened the brown paper wrapping. Inside was a beautiful green velvet cloche with a gold silk ribbon and flower around the brim. The tight-fitting hat had been the style for several years now but Ruby had never had anything but hand-me-downs, and hats were not usually part of the clothing items. Besides her Pa would never have let her wear anything like it. Her eyes filled with tears, and when she looked up she saw that he was grinning at her response. Suddenly, she felt like a child again, even though that was the last thing she wanted to appear to him.

"Thank you, Sal. I really appreciate it. I – I didn't get you anything. I really didn't know if you were ever coming back."

Sal took her hands in his, and said in his lovely Chicago/Italian accent that she so loved, "Salvatore D'Angelo is a man of his word. Did you hear me tell the men on the porch that day that you were mine? I meant it, Ruby. One of these days I'm going to get you out of this joint. A dame – a girl like you should not have to live like this. Will you come with me when I'm ready? You're sixteen, right, the age of consent?"

"Oh, -- of course, yes, I'm sixteen." It was then that Ruby knew she had a way out for sure, away from her brutish father, poverty, gas fumes, and loneliness. "Yes, Sal, I'll go with you, anywhere. Whatever you say."

He picked her up and twirled her around, but when they heard voices exiting the garage, he whispered, "I've got to go. It sounds like their business is done. I'll see you soon."

"I'll be waiting," she whispered breathlessly. He pulled her in for one more lingering kiss, pressing his body tightly to hers, and then he quickly left before the men could see him exit the house. He was standing next to the car when they returned. Under the moonlight, Ruby saw Sal tip his hat in her direction before he climbed in behind the wheel. The moment he left, emptiness set in once more – but this time there was a ray of hope.

≈

At Christmastime a box of clothing had been left on the porch for her. Luckily, her father never objected to these hand-outs. His attitude was, the less he had to spend on her the better. She was able to wear one good dress that was somewhat fashionable. In January, Ruby was on her hands and knees reaching for the clothing box she had placed under the bed, in hopes she could alter another dress to her size. She was in need of some underwear, also, and she was hoping there was something there she could use. Going by touch only, she accidentally grabbed another box she had placed there. It was the hat Sal had given her. She had hidden it from her father, because she knew all too well how he would react. She listened for her father's voice and footsteps and when she detected nothing, she pulled the hat out and lovingly caressed it. In a previous charity box last fall, Ruby had discovered a hand mirror framed in the new Bakelite. Someone must have suspected that she was combing her hair by touch only. She pulled the hat on her head and then looked in her mirror, but just as she had seen before, it was all wrong. Her long hair didn't look right hanging out of the bottom. She tried to stuff her hair under the hat, but it kept falling out, and she didn't have the right type of pins to control it. Suddenly, she was missing Sal so much that there was a pain in her gut. She couldn't wait for him to return, and when he did, she wanted to be ready for him.

She would be sixteen for real in June, the countdown to her legal adulthood was nearing. The thought of Sal taking her away, gave her strength. Inside her head she heard an angry voice, saying, 'I'm not going to take it, anymore.' She slowly walked into the kitchen and retrieved a pair of scissors from a drawer, then she went back to her room and began to cut off her hair. The long locks fell slowly to the floor. Ruby cut it just below the ears in a bob, the way she had noticed that most girls were wearing their hair now. She wasn't sure if it was even in the back or not, but she didn't care. The freedom she felt with each snip of the scissors was exhilarating. When she looked into the mirror, she saw that her natural waves had fallen into place when the weight of her long hair had been lifted. Ruby grinned. At last, she looked like everyone else. She placed her cloche on her head, and saw for the first time what Sal had seen, a real beauty.

"Why," she whispered, "I'm the bees' knees." Then she giggled and did a twirl, but as she did so, she noticed all of the fallen hair on the floor. She silently stared at the evidence of what she had done. Along with that reality came fear; a single tear trailed down her cheek. She quickly grabbed the broom and dustpan, and cleaned up her mess. But there would be no hiding her haircut. And just as she had known would happen, when Earl saw what she had done, he accused her of terrible things, and called her the worst names a father could ever call his daughter. Then he beat her until she was black and blue.

Chapter Twelve

That winter was brutal, so there was very little traffic during the day, except for an occasional farmer, but the deep drifts and swirling white flakes didn't stop the trucks from coming and going in the middle of the night. It was 1931 now and prohibition had been around a long time – for 11 years nationwide and longer in Michigan. Most people drank some form of alcohol but never talked openly about it unless they were sharing it with the closest of friends. Selling bootlegged alcohol was a booming underground business, and, for the most part, on this side of the state it was run by the Chicago mafia. Ruby was constantly worried about being raided, and wondered how she could stay out of it if it ever happened.

She was fully aware that Sal was involved, but she had no idea to what extent. She lay awake at night wondering if he was more than just a driver for the mob. Did he actually take part in rum running himself? Was he ever involved in gunfights? Was he in danger? Would he ever come back for her, and if he did would she go with him? She prayed to God to help her solve her dilemma. She was sure God did not approve of the illegal alcohol business, but what about her? Did he approve of her father's drunkenness and brutality toward her? Had God ever been there to help her when she had called out to Him? More than once, she woke up with a tear-stained face. She had resolved that as soon as she turned sixteen, if Sal did not come back for her, she would leave on her own. Her father couldn't force her back then. She didn't know where she would go, but maybe that nice lady at the store in town would give her a job and help her out. But for now she knew one thing -- if she had to beg and steal to get out of this hellhole, she would.

As the snow began to melt away, and the purple and yellow crocuses popped up through the white flakes that were left behind in small piles, the world took on a fresh new look. At that exact same time, Ruby's life took a turn. It was early March, a time when it could be winter one day and spring the next and then it could quickly turn back to winter. On one of the mellow fifty-degree days, a car came down the road, bouncing in the ruts and splashing mud along the way. As always Ruby glanced out the window to see who and what kind of vehicle had arrived. A very dirty 1929 Model A Ford pulled up to the pump. It wasn't any different than most, so she went back to her sweeping, making sure she retrieved every last crumb and fleck of dirt so as not to set off her father's wrath. The linoleum was so old that most of the pattern had disappeared; sweeping was getting more difficult as the broom bristles would often stick to the part of the flooring that had worn away. Ruby was wondering to herself what Earl did with his money. He must be paid well for acting as a way station for the booze that came in and out, but she certainly never saw any of it.

She could hear soft conversation as the man who needed gas and her father chatted, and then when the transaction was over, Earl went back to his garage wiping his hands on the rag that hung out of his back pocket. Ruby was bent over the dustpan when there was a soft knock on the door. Startled, she almost dropped her dirt all over the floor. She was a little perturbed, because redoing her work was the last thing she needed. She could never keep up with the daily chores. She often wondered why she worried about it because nothing she did ever satisfied her Pa, anyway.

Ruby carried the dustpan with her to the door, but when she opened it, she dropped the dirt without another thought. It was her Sal, standing there in broad daylight.

"Sal! What are you doing here? Pa's just on the other side of the lot."

"Well, that's a fine howdy-do. Aren't you glad to see me?" To Ruby, he looked like a movie star in a magazine -- dark eyes, perfectly groomed dark hair, and oh so clean.

Ruby quickly pulled him in, then shut the door. She wrapped her arms around him, kissing him softly, while taking in the manly scent of fresh pine and his Brylcream, pomade. He laughed, relieved with her greeting. They had not seen each other since just before Christmas, when he had given her the hat, and even though Sal came off as very sure of himself, he was so taken with Ruby that he was always worried she would change her mind about him. He was, after all, in a very dangerous business.

Sal pulled her in tighter, for a longer chance to sample her lips, and it was then that he noticed there was more roundness and firmness to her chest. She was taller by an inch or so; he liked the way she fit to him now. His hands roamed from her back to the fabric of her breast; she was startled and pulled back. "My, my. My little Ruby has grown up," he said when he discovered what was beneath.

"Stop," she giggled, as she slapped his hands away. "Pa will come in any minute. Why are you here? Did he see you come in?"

"Oh, your pa knows all right. I paid him a little extra."

"What? He took money from you, for me? Did he plan to sell me to you for the afternoon or just for an hour?" Ruby was furious and backed away from Sal. She moved to the other side of the room, horrified that he would think she would agree to such an arrangement.

"No, baby doll," he said softly. "I just needed to buy some time with you, and he took the money eagerly. Please listen to me."

Ruby was now crying, and unashamed to be doing so in front of him. She wondered what her mother would have thought of this situation, and what was in her father's head. But worst of all was her Sal. She couldn't understand what she had ever done to make him think she was one of 'those' girls.

"Ruby, listen for a minute. I think you're misunderstanding the situation. Yes, I paid your father for a roll in the hay with you, and he took it. What kind of a man does that make him? But I never had any intention of – you know – well, you know. I was buying time, and that's all. Okay?"

Ruby couldn't help but relent as she looked into his eyes. They were so concerned for her. "Okay," she said quietly. "What do you need to talk about?"

"Can we sit on the sofa? I want to tell you about myself."

"Sure."

Sal sat as close to Ruby as he could, and he held her hand while he told her his history and his connection to the famous Al Capone. "I've been working with him since I was a kid. I shined his shoes one day, and he took a liking to me. He said I reminded him of himself at that age. I had been on my own, living on the streets for a while, selling newspapers, and shoveling horse manure – anything to get by. For some reason Mr. Capone decided to take me under his wing.

He's really not a bad guy, well, not all the time. He has a heart of gold if he likes you."

When Sal saw that he had Ruby's complete attention, he continued on. "I've worked for Mr. Capone for over nine years already, since I was eleven years old. He trusts me. So when he wanted to buy a house on White Lake, he put it in my name. He said it was payment for a job well done. Now this house might be in my name, but that's only because Mr. Capone never puts his name on any title. He owns houses all over the state of Michigan, but only one is in his name – the one in Escanaba."

Eager to know everything, Ruby asked, "So what does he do with these houses?" She was so taken in by Sal's story that she wanted him to tell her all.

"Well, in this case, he wants me to live there, and take care of the grounds. Make it look like anybody else's place, you know? But then – well, you know all about your father's dealings with Mr. Capone's people?"

"Yes, I've figured it out along the way."

"Well, I would have to manage the same type of business. You see, the rum and other bootleg liquor coming in from Canada makes a stop here, because Mr. Capone and the Purple Gang have an arrangement."

"An arrangement?"

"Yes, -- and Ruby I should not be telling you any of this, but I have to, to get my point across. The Purple Gang works the east side of the state, and Mr. Capone gets the west side. U.S. 131 is their dividing line. Neither gang can do business on the other's side. But because of the position of Shaeffer's, your father is able to be a transfer spot or way station. The booze is smuggled across from Canada near Detroit, dropped off here by the Purple Gang, and then picked up by Mr. Capone's men. Usually, it's distributed across the state and then to Indiana and Illinois, by truck. But that's getting too dangerous, now. The Feds are on to us."

"But how else can it be done?" asked Ruby, completely drawn into the scenario, now.

"Mr. Capone has a boat that will run the Lake Michigan shoreline. The house I'll have is at Wabaningo. Have you ever heard of it?"

"No, where's that?"

"It's actually a small settlement on the western end of White Lake, right on the White Lake Channel which feeds to the big lake. It's a perfect location. And the house is surrounded by deep woods. They can drop the anchor for the larger boat in Lake Michigan and then take a dinghy through the channel and pick up the hooch from my house."

"But won't that be dangerous for you?" Ruby was seeing that Sal could be in real trouble, and it was becoming very worrisome to her.

"Well, not so much for me. I'll just be a house owner to the general public. Sometimes the booze will come across White Lake by boat and sometimes in the trunk of a car or truck. Each time it will be different, so it doesn't arouse suspicion. My only job will be to help unload it when it arrives. There's no one out there to see us, anyway. Now, here's the question. Will you run away with me? I have a job. It's good pay, and now I have a house and the use of the car. I can get you out of here, Ruby. And best of all you're legal age, and your father can't come after us. Even if he did, Mr. Capone would interfere."

Ruby gasped. "You mean he knows about us?"

"Of course, he knows. I could not do this without his permission. And besides, he wants us to be a normal husband and wife to avoid suspicion. Oh Ruby, I love you so much. We can make this work. And when prohibition is over – and it will be one day soon – we'll have a house of our very own. Mr. Capone promised it would be ours forever. What do you say? Will you come with me today?"

"Today?" She was startled at his request, but Ruby saw in one quick flash that the answer to her prayers was right in front of her. She was also aware that she had only been with Sal on a few short occasions over the past year. She had no intention of going from the frying pan into the fire. "I need to know something, first. Do you kill people, Sal? Are you truly one of Al Capone's men?"

"Ah, Ruby, is that what you think of me? Have you ever heard any of the men call me by my nickname?" Ruby shook her head no. "It's 'The Angel' for D'Angelo, my last name, but they also call me that because I refuse to carry a gun. They still look at me as an innocent kid under Mr. Capone's protection. In reality, I'm only a driver. I will not let you be a gun moll. I promise."

Ruby sat still for a moment as many confusing thoughts rolled through her head. She was still only fifteen, and wouldn't be sixteen for a few months yet, but Sal didn't know that. Could she pull it off? She really did love him, that much she knew -- her heart raced whenever she was around him and her dreams were filled with nothing else. But then she had never known love in any fashion, so she wasn't sure if it was the real thing.

Salvatore D'Angelo, a twenty-year-old active mob member for Al Capone sat on the sofa holding his breath while his naïve fifteen-year-old beloved made a decision about their lives. Ruby saw his tension and instantly knew that any man that cared for her that much was worth the chance. "Salvatore," she said softly, "give me a minute to grab my hat, and then I'm coming with you."

Sal kissed her so hard, she thought he would break a rib. Then he laughed out loud, and did a little whoop. He kissed her face all over and touched her beautiful short cut hair, which he had neglected to notice until then, because all he had was love in his eyes. He promised to give her the moon, and she cried knowing he meant every word.

With the few meager possessions she owned tossed in a pillow case, and her green velvet hat planted firmly on her head, she hopped in the black model A while her father watched helplessly as they drove away. Legal age or not, he was not about to go against Al Capone.

Chapter Thirteen

From the time Sal first whisked Ruby away from her miserable life, nothing was ever the same for her. They drove straight to a Justice of the Peace who had been placed on standby in case Ruby agreed to get married. Sal had also thought about needing a witness or two, so he had asked a man in his 'circle of friends' and his girl to be waiting to greet the couple. Ruby was a little afraid of the man named Duane; there was an obvious bulge of a holstered gun beneath his jacket. His moll, Marie, was a gum-chewing, bleached blonde with ruby red lips, but they were both friendly and excited for the couple. The Justice of the Peace took one look at Ruby and knew she was most probably not yet sixteen, a fact to which Sal had been blind, but with a little 'persuasion' from one of Mr. Capone's best, he agreed to go ahead with the ceremony.

Ruby couldn't believe this was all happening. The most handsome man she had ever seen wanted her to be his wife. She would never have to go back to the gas station again; in fact, she resolved to never even see her father for the rest of her life. That part of her life was over, and she would wash it out of her memory as if it never existed. She had no mother or siblings, and if there were any grandparents, aunts, or uncles, she had never known them or been told about them. So she was free – free to start a fresh new life. She promised to be the best wife Sal could ever imagine. She would never forget her good fortune.

After the ceremony, Sal took her straight to their love nest at Wabaningo. The winding road which followed the shores of White Lake was gorgeous. And when the little model A jounced down the rutted road toward Wabaningo, Ruby was in awe. The area was thick with trees and barely settled, with only a few cottages scattered here and there. The house that was to be theirs was a small, unassuming, white clapboard, bungalow. Many of the same style single-storied houses with front porches were seen in lake areas. They would blend right in and become one of many couples starting a life together, which is exactly as Al Capone, himself, had planned it.

"Here it is. What do you think, doll face?"

"Oh, Sal, it's perfect. It's *too* perfect, in fact." Ruby asked breathlessly, "Are you sure we're in the right place?"

Sal reached in his pocket, and dangled the keys. "We sure are, and here are the keys to our little paradise. Mrs. D'Angelo, would you care to join me inside?" Sal was almost shaking with eagerness to get his lovely bride behind closed doors and all to himself.

"I'd love nothing better," Ruby replied.

Sal jumped out, ran around to her side of the car, and opened the door. Then he took her hand and led her to their love nest. Ruby held her breath as he carried her over the threshold, almost afraid of what was to come next, but wanting it so badly at the same

146

time that she ached. Sal placed her feet gently on the floor and wrapped his strong arms around her, kissing her the way a man should kiss his wife, with no fear that they were doing something wrong or that they would be discovered by Ruby's overbearing, brutal father.

"Baby, I can't wait to seal this deal, if you know what I mean," he said breathlessly, "but first I need to tell you something. I want to make sure you know what you're getting into, here."

Ruby was more than ready to 'seal the deal' and a little disappointed that they had stopped what they were doing, but she nodded weakly. Sal led her to the sofa, their sofa Ruby realized, as she glanced around at the already furnished house. Everything was brand new, clean, and pretty. The floors were polished and the kitchen sparkled and gleamed. The house was small and open so you could see from one room into the next – all except the bedroom, which had a closed door. Ruby was eager to see what was on the other side, but apparently Sal had other plans. She tried to be patient as her new husband held her hands and looked at her with a love she had never felt in her entire life. At that moment she knew in her heart, she would never do anything to jeopardize what she had.

"Okay, go ahead, Sal." She wound her arms around his neck. "Make it fast. I can't wait to – well, you know." She was sure she must be blushing the color of a tomato, but she didn't care.

"Oh, doll, you make this so difficult for me. But I want you to pay close attention, and if you want out, I'll agree."

Ruby could see that this was very serious, so she pulled back and listened to her new man.

"Out? What do you mean?"

"I explained a little before we left the gas station. But I need to fill you in on more. Mr. Capone would not allow me say anything until you were my wife."

"Okay."

"Sometimes when the men come to unload and load the 'goods,' they'll need a meal or something to drink. At those times we'll be expected to be proper hosts. They will never stay overnight, and it won't happen too often or it could arouse suspicion from the locals, but we will have 'company.' And sometimes our company could gather here for a secret meeting, because we're far away from inquisitive eyes. The Feds don't know about this area, yet. That's why this place is so perfect. Now, most of these men are respectful and just doing their jobs, but some are rather uncouth. I'll always be here with you, and you'll be under Mr. Capone's protection, so based on respect and fear of him, no one should ever lay a hand on you. Now, sometimes we'll be asked to hide someone, so if that happens, you *could* be violating the law. That would be considered harboring a fugitive. Do you understand so far?"

"Yes, I think so. But now I'm a little scared."

"Don't be. I'm giving you the worst scenario, just so you'll know. But you see, prohibition can't go on forever, and when it's over, this place is all ours. So there's the gamble. Are you with me? I promise I will lay down my life for yours."

Ruby didn't have to think about what Sal had said for a second. Romance, intrigue, Chicago mob, smuggling illegal booze. She knew she would have a life full of excitement, even if it was on the wrong side of the law, and she would no longer be that drab little girl at the dirty gas station. But there was a cloud hanging over them, and she needed to clear the air.

"Sal, my new husband," she giggled at the sound of his title. Then Ruby took a breath and continued firmly, saying, "I am not going back on my word. I signed on the dotted line, and I will be your wife for now and always, but I, too, have to tell you something."

"You do?"

"Yes, and I hope it doesn't make you want to tear up our marriage papers."

"Ruby, what could be so awful that I would do that?" Sal was now the one who was concerned and frightened. He couldn't bear to lose his sweet Ruby.

"Well, I haven't been truthful with you about my age. You see, I'm still fifteen." Ruby hung her head in embarrassment.

150

"You are? Well, when is your birthday?"

"In three months. June 10th."

Sal broke out laughing. "Three months? That's nothing, baby. Who cares?"

"But we're illegal. Can our marriage be annulled?" asked Ruby. "I've heard of that happening when an angry father comes after the newly married couple."

"Do you think your father is ever going to come after you? And beside he wouldn't dare, because Mr. Capone gave him enough money to shut him up, if not he'd take care of it permanently, I know that much for sure. And I don't give a hoot about illegal; I'm in an illegal business. But maybe since you're just a little girl yet, I should sleep on the couch for three months, what do ya say?" he said with a twinkle in his eye.

"Oh, Sal, I don't know about you, but I could never last that long." And this time it was Ruby who pulled her husband in, placing her sensual lips on his, feeling his heat and molding their bodies tightly together. The new couple slowly rose and walked hand in hand to the closed door that was to be their sanctuary, the place no 'guest' would ever be allowed to enter. Ruby had never been happier in her entire life. She whispered a silent prayer to God for finding a way out of her awful life, and also gave thanks to Mr. Al Capone for his generosity.

Chapter Fourteen

Over the next week, Ruby and Sal discovered everything about each other, things most couples knew before getting married. They lay awake all hours into the night, talking in the dark, while holding hands and caressing each other, sharing their darkest secrets. They giggled and tickled like children, and made love like adults. Ruby had never in her life had a chance to be a child, so being a grownup housewife in her own home seemed perfectly normal. Sal was pleasantly surprised to learn that his wife had a talent for cooking, something her father had never appreciated. She was also skilled at cleaning house and doing laundry. He couldn't believe his luck, and his joy was overflowing.

They took walks on the beach, even though the days were still cold and damp, then they sat on the new dock wrapped up in thick blankets staring at the stars. They discovered a new rowboat left for them, but it was still a little too chilly to take it out. And then, after two weeks of uninterrupted bliss, they heard the rumble of a car engine coming up their drive. It parked right out in front of the little house, and two men stepped out, both nicely dressed in pin-striped suits with vests and ties. They each wore the standard wool homburg hat; although one of the hats was black and the other a light tan. As Ruby looked out the window, she was embarrassed to see one of the men relieving himself on a tree, after which they approached the door and knocked loudly.

Sal signaled to her, and said in a whisper, "This is it. Just act normal."

When he opened the door to greet them, there was a lot of backslapping and teasing about him being a new husband. Sal introduced the men to his new bride as Hank the Bear -- obviously so-called because of his size -- and Bernie Shortcake, because of his sweet tooth. No last names were ever used. The men were much more

154

polite than Ruby had expected. She served them some coffee and newly made cinnamon rolls that had just come from the oven. When the pleasantries were out of the way, Sal asked Ruby to go to the bedroom and close the door while they conducted their business. She heard words like shipment, hooch, and The Big Fellow, another name for Al 'Scarface' Capone. As Ruby held her ear to the door, she heard them talk about setting up a schedule for delivery. Sal was told when to expect the bootlegged liquor and who would be picking it up. They said it was a little difficult to use this route yet, but as soon as they were sure that the lake was completely thawed when the truck arrived, they would begin to transport through this waterway route. Then Ruby heard furniture being moved and scraping on the floor, but she couldn't tell what was happening. She stayed in her room until the men left and as soon as the car engine rumbled down the road, Sal opened the door and told her it was okay to come out.

"Are you okay, Ruby?"

"Sure, but I was frightened for you."

"There's not a thing to worry about. We're all just doing the job that Mr. Capone asks of us, and as long as we follow along with everything he expects, then there won't be a problem. Our organization runs like clockwork."

"Then why do I have to hide?"

"Well, there are some things you're better off not knowing, in case you were ever questioned by the Feds."

"The Feds? Would they think I was involved?"

Sal kissed her nose and pulled her in tight. "Not as long as you only tell them as much as you're supposed to. For instance, today these men were just asking for instructions. They got lost, right? You never saw them before, okay?"

"All right," she said slowly. "I get it, but what about the others?"

"Well, we just hope the Feds never catch on to what is going on, here. And by the way, the men loved you. You made a big hit with the cinnamon rolls. Do you know how to bake other things?"

"Sure, I can bake pies, cakes, and cookies. I'm great with an apple pie. Sweet goods were the only thing that ever made Pa happy."

"Great. From now on, always keep something freshly baked on hand just in case someone shows up — even if we have to throw it out if it goes stale. Because I think as soon as the spring thaw is complete, we can expect more visitors."

Then Sal took both of Ruby's hands in his and said, "Ruby, honey, you were great, and the men said you passed the test, so now I can show you more. But this next part, you can never share with anyone outside of our 'circle of friends.' Do you understand? It's very important."

"Okay. Sure I can do that. Anything for you, Sal," she said, kissing him gently.

Sal grinned, and then quickly began moving the kitchen table. Ruby realized that must have been the furniture sounds she had heard. He lifted the braided rug and exposed a cellar door.

"Why, I didn't even realize that was there. Where does it go?"

"Come. I'll show you."

Sal went first, lowering himself down the steps that were more like a ladder, and then reached up a hand to help guide Ruby down. She carefully placed her feet on the open slats, thinking she was probably going into a fruit cellar used for storage, but what she saw instead, shocked her.

"Stop right there a minute. Let me light this lantern." As the match hit the wick, the place began to glow, but only out a few feet in front of them. It was enough for Ruby to tell that there was a hallway or tunnel of some sort. Ruby was able to detect a few shelves on the side wall with canned goods and some bottles of liquor, probably waiting for transport, but not much. Maybe it was meant for Sal's personal use.

"What is this? Where does it lead?"

"Come with me. Here, hold my hand. I'll show you."

The tunnel was neatly carved out into the earth and supported with strong wooden beams along the side walls and overhead. It was well-made and seemed safe, but smelled dank and musty, created from the underground dampness seeping in. Ruby could see that this structure didn't happen overnight, and certainly was not made just for her and Sal. They walked about fifty feet, and then Sal came to a stop. Ahead of him was another set of stairs. He began to climb up and worked a lever to open the hatch and then raised himself up. Looking cautiously around, he reached back down for her hand.

When Ruby poked her head through the opening, she was surprised to see that they were in the garage and workshop.

"Why, I would never have guessed that we would come out here. But what's this all for?"

"Well, honey, there will be times, and I hope not often, when one of the men is running from the law. He might have to pull his car in the garage to hide it, but before he does, we'll open the hatch, let him down the tunnel, and push his car over the opening. And once in a while, if one of Al's men is already in our house, when someone comes over we weren't expecting –

"You mean, the law?"

"Yes, the law – then we'll let him go down under our table and hide him in the tunnel until they leave. It will be our job to keep the tunnel well-stocked, clean, and ready for a lengthy stay, if need be."

"Oh my, I'm not sure I'm up for that."

Sal's eyes narrowed. His body tensed, and his voice was firm. "Now, Ruby, you said you knew what you were getting into. We're in it now. We have no choice."

Ruby had never seen Sal even slightly angry. She backed down immediately, saying, "Yes, yes, of course, you're right. I'm just surprised, that's all. This is new to me. Give me a little time to adjust, okay, hon?"

When she saw the grin reappear on Sal's handsome face, she knew it was going to be all right. "Now," he said, "let's go back down and continue. Are you ready?"

They carefully lowered themselves once again, and then followed the tunnel for more than twice the distance than before. Ruby was beginning to be apprehensive about being under ground for so long with no way out. But just when she thought about asking Sal to turn back, they came to another set of steps. This time she eagerly went up, anxious to leave the damp earthen hallway and suck in fresh air. And once again, she was shocked to see where she was. They were standing in the boat house, down by the water's edge.

"Oh, my. I'm assuming this is one more way in and out of our house."

"Yes, it's an escape from our house to the boat, in case someone is on the run and this is also how we'll move the hooch from the trucks to the boats."

"That's not very secure," said Ruby thoughtfully. "Wouldn't someone be able to enter our house without us knowing about it, in the middle of the night?"

"Yes, I suppose they could. But remember what I said. This house might be in my name, but it's not really mine. Mr. Capone or one of his men pull all the strings. We just live here and do what we're told."

Ruby was silent a moment. Could she really live like this? And if the answer was no, could she give up Sal? Sal could tell she was turning everything she had learned around in her mind, trying to make a decision. He held his breath until his lungs ached, hoping for the answer he so needed to hear. But when Ruby faced her feelings, she knew without a doubt that giving him up was unthinkable. He was her rock and her lifeline. And with that conclusion, she also knew that she had no choice but to stay and follow through with what she had promised – 'to love and obey, 'til death do us part.'

Chapter Fifteen

Life was fairly uncomplicated in the spring of 1931. Trucks, cars, and men came and went, and Ruby performed her duties as a hostess, baker, waitress, and sometimes even as a seamstress when an article of clothing was torn and needed repair. Everyone loved her, especially Sal. He was so proud of her at times he thought he would burst.

The tunnel operation was running smoothly. They had it down pat, and no one in the town seemed any wiser. Ruby never saw Al Capone other than that one time at the gas station; his trusted soldiers took care of all of the details, and as long as he was in charge, they never outstepped their bounds. Then, in June of 1931, three things happened. The first was when Ruby turned sixteen, and finally felt like her marriage was legal.

They celebrated by going to a speakeasy that Sal knew about. Ruby had never been out dancing with Sal and was pleasantly surprised that he could cut a rug. At the end of the evening he presented her with the most beautiful necklace she had ever seen – something fit for a queen. He opened the velvet lined box and proudly handed it to her. It held something, that just last year, Ruby would have thought was unattainable for a girl like her -- a sparkling ruby and diamond necklace.

"Rubies for my Ruby," he said, apprehensively. He wasn't sure how she would react to his thoughtfully romantic gesture.

"Oh, Sal, I've never seen anything like this before. Is it real?"

"Of course, it's real. Here, let me put it on you." He fumbled with the clasp as Ruby studied her reflection in the mirror. The necklace consisted of five large rubies, each surrounded by diamonds. It laid flat to her chest in the shape of a V, which accented the hollow of her throat.

Ruby ran her hands over the rubies, tears filling her eyes. "This can't possibly be mine. Why, where will I ever wear such a thing?"

"Don't worry, babe, as soon as prohibition is over, we can begin to live the high life. We can go dancing every night. We can move to the city and get a big house, and we'll be invited to all kinds of fancy parties. You'll be the belle of the ball."

"Such dreams. Could it be true? But what would we do with our house here?"

"We'll keep it as a summer cottage, like the rich people do. And we'll fit right in. I have lots of money that I've been afraid to spend. So, do you like it, the necklace?" Sal gazed at his beautiful bride with her finger-waves tightly curled to her head. Her eyes were as large as saucers and swimming with tears. He caressed her neck as they both admired the rubies in the glass, and then his hands began to travel lower following her contours and curves. She sighed and bent her head backward to his chest as he gently nibbled one earlobe. He noticed a fullness to her breasts and a roundness to her belly that wasn't there before. Gone were the sharp angles of her youth. She was truly becoming a woman, soft and rounded, and it excited him to new heights. Ruby, too, was far more passionate than she had ever been, and all the while she wore her rubies and diamonds over her naked body while they made love. Later, tangled in the sheets and exhausted, Sal remarked that the rubies must have special aphrodisiac powers. Neither one had ever been more sexually free than they had on that night. From that day on, Ruby wore her necklace on special occasions, whether to celebrate her birthday or Sal's, Fourth of July, New Year's Eve, or whatever excuse they could come up with. Sometimes it was for no reason at all. Sal would wink at her and say, "Can you wear the necklace, Ruby?" And her heart would flutter with anticipation.

A few weeks after Ruby's sixteenth birthday, the second event happened. Ruby realized that she was pregnant, and had been for a while. She had been afraid to acknowledge it for fear that Sal would say they couldn't afford a baby. But now that she knew they had some security, she was excited to tell him. And much to her surprise, he was over the moon.

And then, thirdly, something unbelievable occurred when Al Capone was indicted for tax evasion. Up until this time he had only served one month in jail for having a concealed weapon in Philadelphia. No others charges had ever stuck. And try as they might, the Feds had been unable to pin the St. Valentines' Day massacre of 1929 on him, since he had been in Florida at the time -- although it was most likely that he had hired the Purple Gang from Michigan to handle the Chicago slaughter of Bugs Moran's gang.

Sal brought home the newspapers daily so they could read the reports. Their new Philco cathedral-style radio was tuned into the news every evening; they sat next to it, eagerly listening in on the events as they unfolded. It seemed that Al "Scarface" Capone, with the advice of his lawyers, had pleaded a deal for two and a half years, but the harsh judge declined it. Capone would stand trial in October for tax evasion. Everything was uncertain now.

Sal was paid very well for his service to the Capone organization, but he didn't often spend money on luxuries. He said there would be plenty of time for that in later years, when any suspicion of bootlegging activities would be off of them. She never went down into the tunnel after that first time. She left that part of their life up to Sal. It would have terrified her to know how much cash was hidden down there at various times.

A month before the indictment, Al Capone had called a meeting of some of his high ranking soldiers. Among them was Sal, although he didn't really fit the bill as 'soldier.' But Mr. Capone wanted him to be there. He had to leave Ruby for a few days to travel to a secret spot in the woods somewhere near Berrien Springs. He had been there before, so it was no problem finding the place. Mr. Capone was in a terrible mood, so most of the men were tiptoeing around him, afraid to say the wrong thing, because he was known for losing his temper in an instant and taking it out on whoever was nearby. He told them the Feds were closing in on him and were looking for any excuse to put him away. He had the best lawyers available and so far had skipped out on all raps, but it was possible the worst could happen. He wanted to prepare them if he was incarcerated. He took a few men at a time in another room and went over some details of his business that only they knew. And then he called in Sal.

Al "Scarface" Capone praised Sal for his loyalty and said he wanted to make good on his promise if he would continue what he was doing even if Mr. Capone was in prison. He would have to follow the orders of the next soldier in line. Sal agreed, and it was then that he was given the deed to the house, and a lump sum of bonus money – a very large lump sum. "For your wife and soon-to-be-kid," he said with a wink. Then with a hearty slap on the back he said with a laugh, "Now get outta here." In October of 1931, Al Capone was sentenced to 11 years in the penitentiary with an

$80,000 penalty. The jury had found him guilty of three felonies and two misdemeanors.

≈

Ruby had never allowed herself to get to know her neighbors. She was afraid of saying too much and jeopardizing their future, but as fall approached and she began to grow larger with child, she realized she would need some help.

One evening after supper, she approached the subject. "Sal, can we talk about something?"

"Of course, what is it, baby? Are you okay? Is there anything I can get for you?"

Sal was so adorable. He couldn't wait to have a child of his own. He had been orphaned at an early age, and then ran the streets until Mr. Capone took him in. He never really had a home life at all until Ruby came into his world. He was eager to see what it would be like to be a family man, and he hoped to please Ruby with being a better father to her child than she had had herself.

"I'm fine," laughed Ruby. "You don't have to be so nervous around me all the time. I'm just having a baby, and it's not even due until late January, by my calculation."

Sal grinned. "And I don't know how we'll be able to wait that long. There's a little person growing in there. One that you and I made together. Isn't that amazing?"

Ruby laughed, "Yes, there is. But when this little person wants to get out, I might need some help. It's all new to me. I've never even been around a pregnant woman and won't have a clue what's happening, let alone what to do about it."

"Well, we can't have anyone out here. What if some of the guys pull up as you're giving birth. The midwife would know all about us, then."

"That's what I was thinking," said Ruby. "I'm thinking I'm going to have to give birth at the local hospital. Usually, only wealthy women do that. Can we afford it?"

Sal agreed. "Of course, baby doll. Anything. You're right, we can't risk it happening here." Sal immediately thought of Al Capone's incarceration and what could happen to them without his protection. He would never let Ruby know of his fears.

January and early February of 1932 were the normal nasty months. Cold, wind, snow, ice -- everything that comes with winter close to the lakeshore happened that year. But on the night that Ruby felt her first labor pains, the sky was clear and it had not snowed in several days. The roads were rutted but passable, and so the journey into Whitehall was uneventful. The doctor had been paid in advance to be on standby for the big event. Ruby's labor was fairly easy considering her age and the fact that it was her first birth. Sal paced the waiting room smoking a cigar and cursing under his breath each time he heard a moan and scream from his beloved. He made a promise to himself never to put her through this again. It was all his fault; he would find a way to stop all future pregnancies. There must be a way. He would never touch her again. That was the answer. But he loved Ruby so much, how could he stay away from her? He needed her like he needed air to breathe.

And then the sound of a baby crying could be heard in the other room, and at the same time his wife was silent. When the doctor came out to tell him all was well, that Ruby was fine, and he was a father to a beautiful little girl, he didn't hear a thing except the news about Ruby. When he was finally allowed in the room, he was shocked to see her with a baby at her breast. The picture of his darling wife looking down at his child almost dropped him to his knees with joy. He had been so focused on Ruby and her pain, he had almost forgotten why they were there in the first place. Ruby looked up at him with tears in her eyes, looking like an angel, a mother at sixteen, four months before her seventeenth birthday.

During the time that Ruby was in the hospital recovering, Sal went shopping for items on a long list that had been written for him by a nurse when she realized these two had not prepared for a baby to go home, at all. And what was worse, neither one of them had a clue how to care for her. She gave Ruby lessons on how to bathe, burp, and diaper a baby. Although Ruby was young, she wasn't the first mother at this age the nurse had seen. It was all too common these days to see girls marrying at the age of seventeen and having babies immediately after. She even suspected the couple had lied about Ruby's age. And they had, because they didn't think it was anybody's business how old she was when she got married. So when they filled out the information for the baby's birth certificate, they altered the dates a little. It didn't matter to them, so why should it bother anyone else. And then finally the day came for Sal to take his precious Olivia Ivy D'Angelo and her mother home. As the model A drove down the road, the threesome were as happy as clams. It was to be the start of a new life for them, but there was one thing they had forgotten about in their euphoria. That life included gangsters, bootlegged liquor, and guns.

Chapter Sixteen

Life in Wabaningo did not change a bit with Al Capone's incarceration; his men simply carried on without him. With a growing sense that prohibition would not last much longer, there was an increase of deliveries, as they tried to wring every last dollar out of their illegal activities. Along with more activity came more heightened awareness of possible trouble. As soon as Ruby and Sal heard the truck rumble down their road, Ruby would pack up the baby and all of her things and hide out in the bedroom until they figured out if it was safe to come out. She would hear boots thumping on her newly mopped floors, then the scrape of the table's legs as someone opened the hatch to the cellar. The sound of bottles clinking, cursing, and grunting could be heard as the men passed crate after crate down to the tunnel. Ruby did not have a clue how the rest of the operation was worked out once they were down below. All she knew was that the illegal whiskey and gin was somehow transported out to the boathouse, and then sometime later in the night, it was moved once again to a waiting boat on the lake.

Once she was told she could come out, she prepared the men a meal, or just served drinks and desserts. They were rough around the edges, but every one of them loved Olivia. She was passed from bootlegger to bootlegger; the baby was bounced and jiggled and tickled and all the while a goon with a big gun stood at the door. Since Mr. Capone was gone, the caliber of men had changed significantly. Ruby was more frightened every day. And one evening, at supper, she brought her concerns up to Sal.

"Sal, I'm just worried about the baby," she explained.

"I know. I am too. But we have never seen anything like what we read about happens in Chicago. This is a quiet, well-run operation. These guys aren't the smartest bunch; they're just trying to feed their families the same as we are."

"Still, Sal, anything could go wrong. We have to leave. I'm afraid."

"Ruby, we can't. We're in too deep. Mr. Capone still calls the shots from prison. He'd get word if I bailed. It's too dangerous to think about."

Ruby's temper flared. "Dangerous?" she yelled. "What could be more dangerous than what we're doing now?"

"Death, Ruby. Death," snarled Sal. "They're not well-known for leaving stoolies behind."

"But we would never tell anybody anything that has gone on here."

"But they don't know that for sure. They would *have* to shut us up," he hissed. When he saw the tears in his love's eyes, he felt horrible that he had been so harsh, but he needed to get the point across. They were in this until the end. Besides it was the only way to keep the house. He had to fulfill his original agreement with The Big Fellow.

As soon as Ruby realized she had taken her demands too far, she relented. She slowly got up from her chair, and stood next to Sal. She could see the torture on his face, as he acknowledge what position he had put his family in. She placed her arm on his shoulder and kissed the top of his head, stroking gently to relax him, and later that night she surprised him, by lying on their bed wearing nothing but her ruby necklace. Once Sal saw the vision that was his and his alone, all worries of the day disappeared.

One night, Ruby was awakened from a sound sleep with a loud bang. As soon as her brain registered the noise to be a gunshot, she jumped up in a frantic daze to check on Olivia. When she was sure that her child was okay, her next thought was of Sal, who was nowhere in the room, and upon checking, she discovered he was not in the house, at all. Normally, she would not worry, because she knew he was most likely helping with the delivery. But this time was different, something was wrong; she could tell. Ruby was not about to leave her baby and go looking for him, so she had no option but to wait for his return.

The silence seemed to last an eternity as Ruby sat in her rocking chair, but then she heard a boat motor far off on the lake. She held her breath until the sound of men running, doors slamming, and the truck driving away from their house vibrated in the air. But still there was no sign of Sal. Ruby sat perfectly still, praying that her man would come in soon; she was unaware of the steady flow of tears running down her cheeks, curling around her jaw, and dampening her nightgown. When she heard steps on the ladder from the cellar, she stiffened with apprehension, not knowing who was coming.

"Sal?" she said softly. "Sal, is that you?"

"Yes, love, it's me." He scrambled up, then lowered the hatch. "Quick, help me to put the table right again." Ruby saw blood on his shirt, and she almost passed out with fear. But knowing the danger, she straightened the rug and helped him put the table in its place, before asking if he was hurt.

When Sal saw her look of concern, he said, "Don't worry. It's not mine. It's not mine. I tried to help, but it was no use. The boat took him away. Poor soul will be dumped in Lake Michigan."

"What happened?" asked Ruby as she helped him strip off his blood-soaked shirt.

"A little misunderstanding that led to stupidity. Here, throw my clothes in the stove. I don't want any sign of blood anywhere. Someone on the lake might have heard the gunshot. The police could be making the rounds already, looking for the cause. Go on, now. I'm going to get some nightclothes on."

As it turned out, their fears were for nothing. No one came to check on them at all. But after that day, Sal carried a gun. The incident had shaken him up much more than he had let on. He had seen his share of bloodshed, but never in the vicinity of his precious loved ones.

≈

And so, with no other choice, that was how life progressed for the rest of 1932 and 1933. No other incident of violence occurred; money came in at a steady flow. As long as Sal was careful to take only his cut, no one complained. In the fall of 1932, the men brought a very heavy floor safe through the tunnel and dropped it in the cellar at the base of the hatch under the table. It took several men and a handcart to wheel it through the long dank hallway. Ruby knew it was there and that it held a lot of money, but had no idea what the combination was and didn't want to know. Ignorance was bliss, in her estimation.

On occasion the young couple would take Olivia into town to make some purchases for new clothing and other needed baby items. Sometimes Sal would allow Ruby to buy herself a dress or two of the newest fashion. He loved seeing her dressed in the best; he could afford to give her even more, but he knew there would be speculation if she suddenly started to look like a Park Avenue socialite. He kept telling himself that someday they would be free, and then he could say he had inherited some money and let the spending begin. He wanted to give his daughter a pony, and send her to the best schools; in other words, he wanted her to have everything he had been denied. And he wanted to take Ruby out on the town and show her off. He was so proud of his beautiful wife.

Whenever Sal had the urge to go against his plan to lay low, the ruby necklace saved him and kept him grounded. Ruby would get dressed up at home with her newest frock. She always chose something low-cut that would show off the necklace at its best, and they would dance in their living room with the radio playing the latest songs, like 'Brother Can you Spare a Dime' by Bing Crosby, which reminded them that there was a depression going on. They felt completely blessed that they were so unaffected by it. Some of their other favorites were 'I've Got the World on a String' which made them feel happy and positive about their future; 'I Can't Give You Anything but Love, Baby' -- they laughed at that one knowing about the stash of money they were accumulating -- and 'All of Me,' which Sal loved to sing to, especially when it came to the line that went 'I'm no good without you.' Sometimes they carried the portable Victrola to the water's edge and danced under the stars on the dock. The moonlight sparkling on the rubies and diamonds was intoxicating for Sal, and often they couldn't even wait to get back in the house for their lovemaking. After the first time, when they had ended the evening with grass and twigs in their hair and bruises from the stones poking in their backs, they remembered to bring a blanket or two. On warm balmy nights, Olivia would sleep in a drawer they had carried out. Tucked in, tightly wrapped up to keep off the damp, she was completely unaware of her parents' passion for each other.

They managed to get through the winter of 1932, and in February of 1933, Olivia had her first birthday. She was the apple of her father's eye. He loved the way she would reach for him, and he never complained when she pulled his hair or even when she had crying jags while she was teething. He took it all in stride. Ruby was a kind and loving mother, and even though she was not yet eighteen years old, she had all the natural instincts for motherhood that God had given her when he created her to be a girl-child. Life was good.

One night, Sal was sitting in his favorite chair by the fire, when he said thoughtfully, "Ruby, did you know that you're going to be eighteen years old tomorrow?"

"Of course, I did, silly."

"Well, what should we do about it?"

"What do you mean," she asked.

"Come here and sit on my lap."

"Oh, Sal, I'm washing Livvy's face right now."

"Well, finish up and then put her down to play. I want to talk to you."

"Okay," she said slowly. Once the baby was settled on the floor with her toys, Ruby walked suggestively toward her husband. "What is it you really want, big man?" she said playfully.

He laughed. "You know me too well, doll. I always want that, but come here. This is something more serious."

Ruby settled in on his lap and wrapped her arms around his neck. She tried to nuzzle his neck and kiss him, but he gently pushed her away.

"I'm serious now, Ruby. Come on, cut it out. Oh, Ruby. You are a little devil," he sighed as he gave in to her needs.

There was silence as the kissing and caresses continued. Finally Sal pushed her away gently and said huskily, "Okay, stop now. I mean it. Ruby, we have to save this for later. We need to talk. Go sit on the sofa, so I won't be tempted again."

Ruby made a childish pout because she knew it would drive him crazy, but she did as he asked.

"We've finally made it to real adulthood," he began. "You'll be 18 and I'm 23. We have a house and a daughter. But we go on day to day at someone else's bidding. There's a lot of talk now about repealing prohibition, and when that happens there might be some chaos as things adjust themselves. The gangsters are not going to be happy at losing their income. They've already started to change course and go full force into prostitution and drugs."

Ruby gasped. She had been living a sheltered life in Wabaningo, and had no idea what was going on in the big cities. "Will they make us take part in any of it?"

"Well, I hope no one tries to push it, because I won't have any part in that. Drinking is one thing, but I'll have nothing to do with drugs and girls. As soon as the amendment is repealed, I'm done. The house is mine free and clear, as per my agreement with Mr. Capone. I have the deed and no one else has a claim on it, but they could try to give us trouble. So I need to teach you to shoot."

"What? Would it come to that? Shooting?"

"It could. And with Livvy in the house, we can't take a chance. We have to be able to defend ourselves."

"What about the tunnel? It's an open invitation to come in."

"As soon as the repeal goes through, we'll seal it up. And once I square away everyone with their pay, we can begin to live our life the way we want to. Ruby, you'll need to know the combination to the safe – in case something should happen to me; otherwise this has all been for nothing."

"What if the Feds come in and demand that I open it?"

"That's what I've been thinking about. I'll make sure there is only a minimum amount of money in there at all times. The rest we hide somewhere else. That way you or I could open it for them and all they would see was a few hundred dollars, and we would be safe."

"Okay, that sounds logical. We can just say it's our own personal savings."

"And another thing, tomorrow you can wear the necklace on your 18th birthday, but that's the last time, until this is all over. Do you understand?"

"What will we do with it?" Ruby wondered.

"We need to find a really good hiding place. Even if the Feds never come, I don't want to risk one of the guys getting greedy. And so far none of them even knows of its existence."

"Sal, you never did tell me where you got it. Did you steal it?"

"No, no. I didn't steal it, but someone else might have. I – I'm not sure. I paid for it, but it might have been hot."

"Why would you take it, then?"

"Because Mr. Capone gave it to me; he wanted you to have it, so he gave me a good deal."

"Oh Sal, are we in trouble?" Now Ruby really was scared. She had worn the necklace for almost two years, and it had always represented their love for each other, but now it seemed tainted.

"Don't worry, hon. No one knows I have it, as far as I know. But tomorrow we celebrate in style, and I teach you to use a gun. Agreed?"

Ruby sat quietly for a few moments wondering what would become of their idyllic life. And then she silently nodded.

Chapter Seventeen

"Don't forget. You have to cock it first."

"Oh, balderdash, I'll never get the hang of this."

"You're doin' swell. We can't really shoot it, or the echo could be heard and the coppers might come a-runnin'. But just remember, if anyone shows up and threatens you and the baby, you take aim and give 'em some lead poisoning."

Ruby bit her lip with concentration as she scrunched up her eye to get a proper aim. "I guess, I would have no problem shooting a copper if it came down to him or my baby."

Sal laughed at the moxy of his little Ruby. She never failed to surprise him.

"Okay, enough practice for one day. I think you've got the hang of it. If need be, just aim in the general direction and pull the trigger."

"Well, let's pray it never comes to that." Ruby had not realized that she had broken out in a sweat until they were all done with her lesson. She sighed as she used her arm to wipe her brow. She didn't think she would ever be comfortable handling a rod, as Sal called it.

They spent the next few days trying to decide where to hide the money. When Sal laid it out on the table and floor, Ruby couldn't believe the amount. It took up a lot of space, and that was a problem. Sal left two hundred dollars in an envelope that was marked as theirs in the safe. The other money used to buy and sell liquor would be a problem, but there was nothing they could do about that. It had to remain in the safe, so the men that came and went had access to it.

Sal pulled up a floorboard in their bedroom under the throw rug. They were able to stash quite a bit in there. But they didn't want it to all be hidden in one place, so they walked around the kitchen, looking for another spot. Under the sink and over the icebox was too obvious. They nixed the whole kitchen idea. The furnishings in the living room were just too sparse to even think about finding a place there, so they moved on to the garage. Sal placed a large stack in an old rusted toolbox that he had difficulty getting open, and then placed a large amount under the rumble seat in the car in a storage compartment that most people didn't know was there.

"That way, if we have to make a run for it and we don't have time to get all of our money, we'll have something," he explained. "Now, let's walk down to the boathouse."

Ruby was carrying Livvy on her hip. The child was unaware of what her parents were doing and was simply happy to be on a walk in the fresh air. "But, Sal, the goons are in the boathouse all the time. Isn't that too obvious?"

"Well, for one thing, they don't have a clue what we're doing, here. And for another, they just want to get in and out before they get caught, so there's no time to go snoopin' around."

The boathouse held a lot of tackle, extra paddles, motor parts, and was basically a jumbled mess. Sal proclaimed it to be perfect for the rest of their stash. He placed some money in a tackle box, buried it in the dirt floor, then he threw several tarps over the top in a disarrayed manner so as to look more natural.

The young couple came indoors exhausted. They were both filthy and Olivia needed to be fed. Sal took the baby and began to wash her up a little while Ruby warmed a bottle, and then heated water for a bath. As soon as the baby was put down for the night, Sal carried buckets of hot water to a large zinc tub they had purchased the previous year and set up in their bedroom. It was not hooked up to running water, but they had arranged a drain pipe on the bottom so it could be easily emptied out into the yard. His eyes were all ready for what he knew would come next when Ruby came out of the baby's room. She was wearing a thin see-through wrap with nothing on underneath; her ruby and diamond necklace lay at the hollow of her throat. Ruby walked slowly toward him while untying her wrap and letting it drop to the floor right before she reached him.

Sal knew this was the last time he would see her in the necklace for a long time, and he wanted to imprint every inch of her in his mind. He pulled her in close for a long kiss, feeling the warmth of her body pressed up next to his, then he reluctantly let her go, and helped her into the tub. He immediately discarded his own clothing, and climbed in behind her. Bathing together was one of their favorite things to do.

"Let's see if we can manage to have a nice birthday party without Livvy interrupting us," he laughed as he nibbled her ear.

"Fat chance," giggled Ruby.

Sal began to slowly wash Ruby's back and then moved his hands to massage her head with thick suds. She loved it when he washed her hair, but she was more eager to finish the bathing and move on to what was to come next. She allowed him to massage her body and then she did the same for him. And soon they could stand it no longer. They rose from the tub and still dripping wet, Sal carried Ruby to the bed. They didn't care or notice that the bedding was getting wet; they needed each other with a passion more than any other time in their marriage. And by the time they had satisfied each other, hours into the night, the bedding had dried of its own accord.

In the wee hours of the dawn, Sal sat up and looked at his perfect Ruby. He wondered how he had gotten so lucky to have his very own family after all of his years of loneliness. When Ruby felt him stir, she opened her eyes. Sal reached over to a package next to the bed, and handed it to her. "We forgot your birthday present," he said with a grin.

Ruby stretched and yawned, exposing her breasts when the sheet fell away, leaving the necklace to flash its magical powers. Sal sucked in his breath, ready for another go, but Ruby was already tearing into the gift.

"It's not much of an 18th birthday present, but I didn't dare spend big money."

"I understand." As she tore away the wrapping, Ruby discovered a framed picture of them both. It was a picture one of the guys had snapped for them on his camera right after they were married. Ruby looked so young, like a child, but still held the wisdom of an adult in her eyes. And Sal had his homburg hat pushed to the back of his head, a lock of dark hair resting on his forehead. He was laughing with the joy of becoming a new husband.

"Oh, Sal, it's perfect." Ruby hugged it to her, saying, "I'll cherish it forever." She leaned in to kiss him, the necklace swinging freely away from her body, and this time, Sal could not control himself.

"Happy birthday, doll face." He tumbled her back to the mattress, and the bedsprings made music to his ears.

Chapter Eighteen

The summer flew by, with no problems, whatsoever. Ruby often took Olivia down to the lake to splash her feet in the water. The baby loved to dig in the wet sand with her new pail and shovel. Ruby and Sal still danced on the dock on occasion under the stars, but without the lovely ruby necklace. They were still so madly in love that even the missing gems could not quell their passion, but it was different now, they were little more reserved; they no longer felt the sense of wild abandonment.

Ruby longed for her necklace, but Sal had hidden it somewhere so it could never be taken from them by anyone. When she asked where it was, he said she was better off not knowing. She knew he would never hide it in the safe, but she had no idea where he had put it.

He kept saying, 'Soon, Ruby, we'll be able to take it out soon.'

And then just before Christmas, on December 5th, 1933, the 18th Amendment to the United States Constitution was repealed. Selling liquor was once again legal. Ruby and Sal heard the news on their radio and were thrilled that the day had finally come. There was dancing in the streets all over America. People were openly drinking in defiance of the government's long restrictions on them. Ruby and Sal were home free.

Just as Sal had predicted, some men approached him about continuing with their smuggling route, but this time they said they would be bringing in drugs, such as cocaine and heroin. Sal refused to take part, an argument took place, and Sal was pushed around a little. The next time they came, the men were prepared to be more persuasive. They beat Sal with brass knuckles and Billy clubs, and left him in a heap on the front porch.

He was ready for them when they returned the third time. Sal stood his ground, with a shotgun at his side. Ruby was hiding in the back of the house with a pistol held in her shaking hands. She had locked Livvy in the closet for safekeeping. As Ruby shivered with fear, pistol in hand and kitchen knife on the table, she heard loud angry voices, then several shots rang out. Car doors slammed, a motor roared to life, and the vehicle sped down the road, kicking up gravel as it went. Ruby laid down the gun and ran to the door, where she found her husband lying in a pool of his own blood. Her screams echoed across the water. She slid to the floor, cradling his bloodied body to her chest. She smoothed his forehead curl back into place and then pulled it back down, as she rocked her handsome Sal into the next world, dead at 23, leaving Ruby D'Angelo a widow at the age of 18.

Ruby came to her senses when Ivy began to cry. She ran to her newly installed candlestick telephone and rang the police. When they arrived she repeated the lines Sal had made her learn, even though at the time, she could not stand to think of a scenario when she might need to use them. She told the police, two drifters came to the door looking for a handout. Sal fed them, but refused to give them money when they demanded it. One of the men tried to force his way in the front door and they struggled. The tall man shot him, and they both ran through the woods. She had never seen them before.

The police were kind and helpful in making arrangements to take Sal's body into town. Ruby was left alone in the cottage with no one to help her or guide her with the many decisions that had to be made. She could barely function. She was lonely, scared, miserable, and confused, but somehow she managed to get through it.

Within a month it began to be clear to Ruby that she could not live so far from town with a small child. She needed supplies for Livvy, food, and the support of other people around her. And most of all she needed to get away from the house that held so many memories, so she took some of the money they had stashed under the floorboards and with what was hidden in the car, she drove to town and bought a small Cape Cod style house. With one more trip to the lake house, Ruby loaded up everything they would need on a daily basis. Feeling secure with the money Sal had left her, she locked up the cottage and moved to town for good.

The people of Whitehall felt sorry for the young widow, and a few kind women took her under their wing. They introduced her to the unmarried pastor of their Lutheran church, Pastor Michael Hanson. He was a tall, blonde Swede -- the complete opposite of her dark Italian Sal, and ten years her senior. She began to attend church regularly, wanting to make sure Livvy had a proper upbringing, which in her view included Sunday school attendance. She had remembered, when she was in grade school, all of the nice girls had attended a church.

The pastor was there for her whenever she needed spiritual guidance – she had so much to learn -- and sometimes he was there, because as a single man, he enjoyed her company. She was beautiful, sensitive, and kind. He felt great compassion when he saw her sadness, and soon his willingness to help her through it aroused more feelings than a pastor should feel for a member of his congregation. Ruby knew what Pastor Mike wanted from her, but she always kept him at arm's length. She did not want any sign of impropriety. She had a life to make for Livvy in Whitehall.

For the next few years, Ruby was a single mother. She would take Livvy out to the cottage on the lake for walks in the woods, and playtime in the water. Mother and daughter were as tight as mother and child could be. Whenever Ruby was at the cottage, she took a little more of the money to help her get by. She was always thrifty so no one ever questioned where she got her funds.

Ruby's friendship with Pastor Mike continued to grow, and after a few years, the congregation accepted them as a couple, even though Ruby never looked at it as a romantic pairing. No one would ever replace Sal; she wouldn't allow it. She told herself she would wait for the day when she could join him in Heaven. She kept the framed picture of them that Sal had given her on her eighteenth birthday prominently displayed, so Livvy would never forget her father and so Ruby would never forget his face which was beginning to fade from her memory.

When Livvy was ten and Ruby had just turned 27, she realized that life was going to be very lonely if she lived a long time, and she finally agreed to one of many of Pastor Mike's proposals of marriage. The congregation was elated – everyone loved Ruby, but Ruby secretly wondered what they would think of her if they knew her past history as the wife of a bootlegger. And what would they think if they knew she had run off at the age of fifteen to get married. And what about the passionate life she had shared with a man who made her ache with longing to this very day whenever she thought about those long sexy nights with him and the ruby necklace.

Eventually, after Ruby had been married for a year, she agreed to take her husband out to the cottage on the lake. He had always known of Ruby's summer retreats with Livvy, but never wanted to intrude on her previous life. He was an avid fisherman and had asked multiple times if they could go there, and finally she reluctantly gave in. Mike knew her first husband had been killed there, as did the whole town, but he was unprepared for the change he saw in Ruby's eyes when they arrived. She was a completely different person – quiet and wistful. They stayed for the weekend, but much to his dismay, Ruby would not let him touch her in bed. She pleaded a headache and turned her back on him.

The money had long ago been spent for daily living, except for the last bit hidden in the boathouse. Ruby had decided to keep that back for an emergency. And of course, her husband knew nothing about it. It was for her and Livvy and no one else. Mike enjoyed the fishing and caught lots of perch which he prepared for their dinner. After that first day, he often took his step-daughter out in the boat with him. He loved swimming and splashing in the water with Liv, as she now preferred to be called. The trio settled into a quiet life, and Ruby adjusted to her new role as a pastor's wife.

Whenever the pastor needed time away, they used the cottage, but never once did Ruby and Mike ever make love there. He tried to question her once about her life with Sal, but when he saw the pained look in Ruby's eyes, he decided to never bring it up again and let her past be her past.

And then after 25 years of marriage, Pastor Mike suffered a heart attack and left Ruby a widow for the second time. Ruby had never told her complete life story to anyone, except one day when Liv was an adult woman with a child of her own, and was questioning her heritage. Ruby was older now, all of 57 years of age. She began to reminisce, and found herself enjoying talking about Sal. What difference did it matter now. Sal was gone, and Mike was gone. Prohibition was long over. So she told Liv about the bootlegging operation – only the part about the tunnel and the trucks that arrived day and night full of cases of gin and whiskey from Canada, how it was handed off to the Purple Gang and then to Al Capone's men. The rest was lightly glossed over, and no mention of how her father had actually been killed was ever spoken.

At some point the story was passed down through Thomas -- Liv's son – and to Ivy, and laughed about at dinner tables when Ruby wasn't around. 'Grandma was a gun moll,' they would say. 'GG was a flapper.' 'Who knew,' they would shrug. 'That sweet old woman sold hooch. And a pastor's wife at that!'

So that is where Ruby's tale ended, all she had ever wanted to tell anyway, until the day she decided to tell the truth for Sal's sake, so the world would know about a man who loved his wife and child more than life, itself. He was a man who would do anything to provide for them and to protect them, and in doing so, he had paid the ultimate price.

208

Part Four – Ivy

Chapter Nineteen

It was a perfect Sunday for a drive along White Lake. The early June day was tempting Ivy with glimpses of her favorite season. She slowly ambled around the curves and bends of Lakeshore Dr. as she headed towards Murray Road and Wabaningo, excited to get to her destination, but apprehensive at the same time. There were a few sailboats lazily cutting the waves, their white sails in stark contrast to the indigo sky. Ivy had taken this road many times. Her GG often held family gatherings at the cottage over weekends and holidays. Before her father had left her in Olivia's care to go to California and his new life, her great-grandmother, her grandmother, Thomas, Ivy's mother

Julia, and Ivy would spend every 4th of July at the cottage, roasting hot dogs over an open fire and later eating melted and sometimes blackened marshmallows before watching the fireworks over the lake. Then a sleepy Ivy would be carried in her father's arms to the cottage where she would be placed on a cot in her Nana's room.

As Ivy came to a stop in front of the house, she took the time to look over the exterior. It was quite a bit different than it was when she was a child. She remembered the day when GG had pointed out to her the parts of the cabin that were original. A new guest room and another bathroom had been added on in the '50s right before her husband, Mike, had died. And they had screened in the front porch, so they could enjoy hot sticky summer evenings out there, bug-free. Ruby had put up a fuss about the renovations, she told Ivy. She didn't like changes, but Mike had convinced her they needed more room, since they hosted parishioners there on occasion. After Mike died, Ruby had moved back to the lake property permanently, where she could once again feel Sal's presence. It was a very special place, she told Ivy, and someday it would be hers, if they took care of it.

But that was not to be the case, it seemed. After Ruby died, the will was read which granted all rights to the cottage and its contents to Ivy, but before she had a chance to take her claim, she received a letter from the State of Michigan placing a lien on the house. Since Ruby had lived to such a ripe old age, her savings had long ago run dry, but she had still needed to make payments to Red Pine for her care, so many years ago, Ruby had been placed on the Medicaid program, which covered all of her expenses. But after death, the state and federal governments expected reimbursement for whatever they could recoup with any personal property they could get their hands on – in this case, Ruby's house. And since the taxes had not been paid for three years, unbeknownst to Ivy, the City was about to take it over. Ivy had consulted an attorney, but there seemed nothing she could do but pay the back taxes which was way beyond her budget. And even then, he told her, the

State would get their cut, anyway, which was way more than the value of the house. In other words, Ivy was to be left with nothing. She was allowed to take small personal items out, but she was required to leave anything of value behind. Since there were no power tools, and Ruby did not own a car any longer – she had not driven in years – Ivy was told she could clean out the building before it went up for auction. After consulting a lawyer, she discovered that the State moved at a snail's pace, so the actual auction might not take place for months or maybe even a year. In the meantime, the house would sit and rot away, losing its value as it sank into disrepair, waiting for a new owner -- so typical of big government. The whole concept made Ivy sick.

Ivy had received another letter yesterday stating that the inspector would be out to the property to assess its value in three weeks. Ivy was determined to get anything she wanted out before it was too late. She walked slowly up to the door, key in hand. Ivy opened the screen door to the porch and stood there a moment, now for the first time, visualizing Sal's body where Ruby had found him after he had been shot. How had GG managed to stay in this place, with that picture in her mind? As she opened the interior door, a complete picture of what life must have been like in the 1930s was before her. Looking through new eyes, she could envision a romance that was far beyond anything she had ever dreamed of for herself. Ivy sighed deeply, wondering if she would ever find that kind of love.

Trailing her fingers over each piece of furniture, she could see Sal as if he were in the room with her, calling Ruby to sit on his lap. She could imagine them dancing closely as he hummed 'I Can't Give You Anything but Love, Baby' in her ear, and when she entered the bedroom, the hairs stood up on her arms. The passion Ruby and Sal had felt for each other was palpable here, free floating in the air. It could be felt in the rays of sun streaming through the window with the dust particles floating like jewels. It could be felt in the wrought iron bed frame that glowed with a patina that came from being lovingly polished. And it could be felt in the cabbage roses on the wallpaper in their various shades of pink to red that Ruby had carefully chosen and never replaced, faded as it was. Ivy thought she could almost reach out and touch the young couple as they made love on the bed. Her hand moved to touch the quilt that had always been there – a beautiful Double Wedding Ring pattern of various shades of reds with lighter colors interspersed throughout. Ivy imagined it was meant to symbolize Ruby and Sal entangled together in eternal bliss, as they most likely were now that Ruby had at last joined Sal. Ivy turned over the lower corner and read the label. It had been done by Ruby herself in 1932. Ivy had no idea she had known how to quilt.

On the side table was a black and white picture of Ruby and Sal. The black decorated glass surrounded their photo and was set off by silver-gilded wood – art deco at its finest. It had always been there but in Ivy's teen-aged self-centeredness she had never taken the time to really look at it. It must be the one that he had given her on her eighteenth birthday. As she studied the picture, Ivy felt as if she were falling into another time. GG was so young and innocent, but a beauty, nonetheless. She was wearing a straight loose shift with a lace collar and drop waist; she had a cloche hat which fit closely to her head. Her bobbed hair showed around the edges of the low brim. Was it the famous green velvet hat GG had told her about? And Sal – well, Sal would have been known as a heart throb if he had been in the movies, even today. He was wearing loose pants with wide cuffed legs, and a jacket that hung casually open, exposing suspenders and a white shirt. His homburg hat was sitting jauntily at an angle, and tipped down low; he was just as Ruby had described him. But there was more to him than his clothing. You could feel his sexuality oozing through the black and white photo. How had Ruby and Pastor Mike slept in this bed for all of those years? She wondered if GG had placed this quilt and picture back on the bed only after Mike had died. Ivy suddenly pulled her hand back, feeling as if she had stumbled onto something very personal. But then her GG had wanted her to be here, she had willed the house to her, knowing what she would find, and how she would feel once she knew the whole story. Ivy understood that her GG's intentions were that she would find someone of her own and continue with her very own love story right here. But now, sadly, that was not to be the case.

Today, Ivy's goal was to look for papers and letters that might give her more insight into GG's story; she needed to remove those before any strangers, who might have heard of the rum-running operation, came nosing around into GG's personal life. The bedroom was the most likely place for boxes of pictures, since there wasn't a lot of cupboard space in the small house. The bedroom closet only contained clothes and shoes -- the shelf above held scarves, hats, and gloves. -- so Ivy knelt on the floor next to the bed, and, looking underneath, she discovered a box of snapshots of her family throughout her childhood and her mother's when Ruby was a single woman, caring for Olivia alone. There were a few pictures of Ruby's second husband Mike, but they were usually with other people. Ruby was absent in most shots. Ivy decided to take the box home so she could study them closer. She thought she might make an album outlining Ruby's life or insert some of the photos in the center of her book.

As she rose from the floor, a board squeaked. It seemed loose under her foot. Ivy pulled back the rug, wondering if this was the board GG had told her about. Age had caused the old floorboards to shrink, so she was able to easily pull the noisy offender up. Ivy was disappointed to discover that the space held nothing but dust bunnies, but upon reflection she should have expected no less. Ruby was broke, after all, and it had probably been many years since she had been able to get down on the floor to retrieve money. But that did bring up another thought.

Ivy rose from the floor, brushed off her knees, and carried the framed photo and the box into the kitchen. Then she looked under the table and lifted an edge of the rag rug with her foot. She hadn't been sure if everything Ruby had told her was the truth, but so far with the photo of Sal and the loose board in the bedroom, her story was ringing true. Ivy gave the table a shove. It was solid oak, and quite heavy, but with persistence, she was able to move the legs off the rug and flip it back. Ivy sucked in her breath. There it was -- a trap door to the cellar. It could be just for fruits and vegetables. It most likely had shelves lining the walls for canned goods, as Ruby had described. Did she dare look down there? She decided to take a further look and make a decision how far she would take it once she peeked in. She pushed and shoved until she had moved the table far enough to allow the door to open. She was disappointed when she saw that it was too dark below to make anything out. She stood up once again and began to search through the kitchen drawers for a flashlight, but when she finally found one, the battery was dead with acid oozing out. She tossed it in the trash. She would not go down in the cellar today, but she made a promise to herself to come back on Saturday and try again. Ivy closed the cellar door, and with a little more effort, she pushed the table back into place and smoothed out the rug. After packing a few pieces of glassware that she wanted to keep as a remembrance of GG, she locked up the cottage and drove home, exhausted but excited for the next trip.

Chapter Twenty

"Are you kidding me?" said Nancy. "You found a loose floorboard *and* a cellar door?"

"Yes, and now I believe everything she said." Ivy had called Nancy as soon as she got home, excited to tell her what she had discovered. "The picture is exactly as she described it. Look."

Nancy studied the framed photo. "My, she really was a beauty, wasn't she? She's so young, here."

"If I'm right, this is their wedding photo, shot at the Justice of the Peace's office. She was only 15 years old; can you believe it?"

"It was a different time then. The Great Depression was in full force, and even though there seemed to be no hope for the future, people still needed to continue on with their lives. A woman needed a man to provide for her, and he needed someone to care for his house. It was that simple. My very own great grandmother got married when she was seventeen."

"Yes, but fifteen? Of course, Ruby lied about her age, and I probably would have, too, to get away from that father of hers," said Ivy.

Nancy sighed. "It was so much more than that, though, wasn't it? It was a love that most of us never get to experience." Then she giggled, "Of course Matt and I have it pretty great, but this story is something else – so romantic."

"Well, anyway. I'm going to keep going through these other pictures and see what comes up. There might be something I can use, here."

"Ivy," said Nancy biting her lip, thoughtfully, "have you thought about the other hiding places? Didn't you tell me they placed the money in smaller amounts around the property?"

"Oh, yes, you're right. I got so wrapped up in the picture and being mesmerized with the whole lover's vibe out there that I totally forgot about that." Then Ivy stopped for a moment, staring, searching for facts in her memory, trying to remember each word her GG had said. She grabbed her manuscript and flipped through the pages. "Here, here it is, the part where she tells me about hiding the money. Pass me that tablet, please. I need to jot this down, again."

"What does it say?" Then Nancy laughed. "You wrote it. Don't you remember?"

"I wanted to make sure I got the details down right. She said they put some in a tool box in the garage, some in the rumble seat of the car, and some they buried in the boathouse. Well, I'm sure the money in the car was used to buy the house in the city, so that's long gone, and as we know the floorboard hiding spot is empty, too. Chances are it's all gone. She most likely needed it to survive when she was alone with a child. She probably used it just like Sal had intended – a little at a time."

"Well, it certainly wouldn't hurt to take a look," added Nancy. "And what about the cellar. Isn't there supposed to be a safe down there?"

"They might have removed it at some time, but even so, I don't know the combination. Even Ruby didn't know it; she said Sal never had a chance to tell her."

Nancy sat up straight and took Ivy's hands in hers. "Ivy," she whispered, not for secrecy but because of her excitement. "What about the ruby necklace? It's yours now. It was meant for you. I'm sure your GG told you her story so you would be able to retrieve what she had left behind. If it's anywhere in that house, you have to find it. If the house goes up for auction, anything left on the premises becomes the property of the new owner. You could lose it all."

"You're right! That necklace is still somewhere in the house! GG never mentioned finding it. Sal never had a chance to tell her where he hid it, and even if she found it, she would have been afraid to wear it. It must be worth a fortune in today's money, but that's not why I would want it. It was the most precious thing that Ruby ever owned in her life. It symbolizes a love that never dies, and according to Ruby it almost had magical powers."

"So, when are you going back?"

"Next Saturday after work. I'll be done with work at noon. But first I have to buy a couple of lanterns; I'm going down that tunnel."

Chapter Twenty-one

The next few days dragged by; all Ivy could think about was Ruby and the cottage. What treasures could she find there, and how many more secrets of Ruby's remained hidden? She did her job by rote, automatically following the same routine she had done so many times before, but all the while she was living in the past with Ruby and Sal, so on her walk to the car from the grocery store, she was oblivious to the handsome man in the hat who was watching her. He had just pulled into his parking spot and was pleased to see the woman he had been trying to contact for months.

"Ivy! Hello!"

Startled at hearing her name called, she glanced up from the almost impossible job of pushing a cart with a stuck wheel, and was surprised to be looking into Sal's dark eyes – no, it was Fox. Rattled to be back into the 21st century, she gasped, and Fox took it as displeasure at seeing him. Not knowing what he might have done to provoke her anger, he decided to be polite and then continue on.

"I'm sorry, did I startle you?"

"Oh, no – I – I just wasn't expecting you to be there."

"You don't looked pleased to see me," he said softly.

Ivy trembled at hearing the timbre of his voice. She had been avoiding Fox for some unknown reason, and now she was ashamed.

"Oh, no, it's not that at all. I was just preoccupied. Sorry."

Fox studied her a moment, before continuing. "I tried to text you and even left some messages on your phone, but you never returned them. Did I do something wrong? I enjoyed our dinner date. I thought you did, too."

Ivy felt ridiculous standing in the parking lot like this with a man she barely knew. A car pulled up next to them trying to fit into a space that was available. Ivy awkwardly tried to shove and push her cart out of the way.

"Here. Let me help you with that." Before she had a chance to answer, his strong hands had locked over the top of hers on the handle, and he was manipulating the groceries out of the path the car had chosen. Ivy felt a small shock of electricity run through her body with the contact. She pulled back quickly, saw the hurt in his eyes, and immediately felt bad.

"Thank you, Fox. I always seem to grab the only non-functioning cart in the store."

He laughed, and his low rumble was music to her ears. "I know what you mean, but I'm afraid I have to tell you that probably half of the carts don't work properly. Look, all you have to do, is give it a bounce or two to release the stuck wheel – like this." He bounced it lightly on the pavement, saying, "Of course, it's better if you do it when it's empty."

"Thank you, again." Ivy smiled at him, now embarrassed about her behavior. He was a nice man who had taken a girl out to dinner, and the least he had expected was a little conversation on the phone afterwards. That was all. In her misery, she had neglected him, and it was no fault of his own. "Fox, I feel I owe you an explanation. Can we meet up somewhere? I don't think this is a good place for a talk."

"Sure." His face lit up with a grin, feeling he had another chance with this incredibly interesting woman. "Just say where and when."

"Same diner? For coffee?"

"Sounds great."

"Okay," she said, "give me an hour. I need to put my groceries away."

"See you there. You're not going to stand me up, are you?" he teased.

"Of course not, I would never do that," she said with a little irritation.

"Just kidding, Ivy. In an hour, then." And he continued on to the store to purchase bottled water and snacks for his motel room later.

≈

When the groceries were put away – everything that needed to go in the fridge and the freezer, anyway – Ivy bent down to scratch Percy between the ears. He closed his eyes and purred softly, then he banged his head on her leg and pushed lovingly over and over.

"I know you're lonely, Perce, but I have to go out again. Sorry. A man named Fox is waiting for me. Don't worry, he's not a real Fox, so no threat to you. Or me, I hope." Ivy continued her chatter as she freshened her makeup and combed her hair. The cat was happy to follow her around, as she lifted clothing left on the couch and pushed aside items on the counters in search of her favorite hair clip. And there it was, in plain sight all along. She swept her hair up and plopped it carelessly in the clip; convincing herself this was not a date, and therefore no extra care was needed. What she didn't realize, and for the rest of her life would never get through her head, was that she was at her best when she wore a casual look. She was a classic beauty, who never needed much attention.

Once again, Fox had arrived at the diner before she did, and was seated at the same booth at the back. He had been watching the door for her arrival this time, and was taken aback with the picture she presented when she entered the room; she was totally unaware of the men who turned their eyes to follow her as she moved across the floor. This time, he rose to hug her and kiss her on the cheek. Ivy was glad he did. She loved his masculinity and lingered, perhaps a second longer than she had first intended. He was glad to see her blush when he released her.

As soon as they were seated, Ginny, the new waitress, approached to take their order. She had seen their greeting, and almost changed direction, feeling that she was intruding on a private moment, but she had a job to do. The boss was watching and rating everything she did. "Can I get you guys anything?"

"Coffee, black, please."

'Of course,' thought Ivy, 'what else would he drink?'

"I'll have my usual mocha decaf. Thanks, Ginny."

"Oh, so you like chocolate," he teased.

"Yes. I guess you could say, I'm a true chocoholic, and proud of it. I even put chocolate syrup on chocolate ice cream."

He laughed. "Doesn't everyone?"

Ivy giggled. "In my world they do." Now that the ice was broken, Ivy felt it was okay to go forward with the reason she had invited him here. "Look, Fox, I wanted to apologize for not returning your calls."

"You don't owe me an explanation. Really. We only had one date."

"Well, yes, but I know you intended to see to me again, and I wanted you to call me – really."

"What happened, then?"

Ivy took a deep breath, "My GG died shortly after we met. And following so closely on the heels of Nana's death, it was almost too much for me to bear." Ivy looked down at her hands and began fumbling with the napkin, folding and folding until it was too small to fold anymore. "I went into a depression, and I couldn't pull myself out. I'm all alone, now, and couldn't bear the thought of it, I guess." Her eyes filled with tears. This is not what she had planned to say, but there was something so sympathetic about Fox that she felt herself telling him all of her feelings during that dark time. He held her hands and listened with compassion as she explained about the early death of her mother and the non-existent relationship with her father.

"So, you see, I'm basically an orphan. There's no one left, but some half-siblings in California that I don't even know."

"Oh, Ivy, I'm so sorry for your loss. I believe I would have felt the same way you did if that had happened to me."

"Well, that's why I didn't return your calls. Not because I didn't want to, but because I was in a place where I could barely function. I don't know where I would be if it wasn't for my best friend, Nancy. She mothered me through it all."

"What brought you out of your funk?"

"It was my GG, herself."

Fox raised an eyebrow in question.

"Nancy convinced me to continue with the book I was writing about GG, in order to stay close to her."

"And did you?"

"Yes, I finished it, and I think it's quite good. I have a little more research to do, and then I might try to submit it."

"Wow, I'm impressed. Good for you." He was grinning from ear to ear at the thought that she had not rejected him; it had been a personal problem, and that's all.

Ivy ate up his praise. For some reason, what he thought about her writing and being an author meant everything to her.

"Can I see you again, Ivy? I'm here for a few days this time. Maybe a week."

"I'd like that."

When Ginny returned with their coffees, she found two people looking exactly like lovers, staring into each other's eyes.

Chapter Twenty-two

Fox and Ivy enjoyed each other's company so much that their coffee date turned into a meal. They each decided to have the special of the day, hot beef sandwiches, with homemade mashed potatoes and gravy. Ivy learned that Fox didn't like traveling for his job, but it was all he had done since he graduated from college. Real estate was all he really knew, and he was good at it. He tracked down available properties all over the state.

At the end of their meal, they finally had to say goodbye, since it was obvious that Ginny was waiting for their table to clear. She had come to their booth a few too many times asking if there was anything else she could get them. When Ivy looked at the clock on her phone, she was surprised to see they had been there for three hours.

"Oh my," she laughed. "I think they're going to charge us rent pretty soon."

"I think you're right." Fox was amazed at how easy it was to talk to Ivy. He had never had such an experience with a woman before. Usually, there was something that got in the way – a difference of opinion on politics, religion, or movies they liked. Even small irritating habits could put a damper on things. But none of that was present with Ivy. It seemed they were a perfect match. Fox needed to see her again. He couldn't explain it, but he did not want to let this woman go. The electricity between them was almost visible. He was ready to ask her back to his motel room, but he could tell she was not that kind of person. And truth be told, he was glad of it.

"When can I see you again, Ivy?"

"Well, I have to work the rest of the week, but I do have a little more free time now that I don't have to visit Red Pine. I didn't know what to do with my routine at first, but now I'm amazed at how I ever managed before. There's always so much laundry and grocery shopping I need to keep up on."

"Well, you got the groceries out of the way today. When's laundry day?" he chuckled. "Can I see you on Saturday? I hear it's supposed to be a nice sunny day."

Ivy thought about her trip to GG's cottage, but when she looked at Fox's handsome face, awaiting her answer, she couldn't say no. "Okay, Saturday it is. I had something planned, but it can wait until Sunday. What do you have in mind?"

"You know, I haven't seen Lake Michigan in this area. I've been wanting to get to the beach, but each time I come over here, the weather is cold and windy. I love the lake on this side of the mitten. You have the best beaches over here."

"We do at that, and proud of it. Should we go to the channel and see the lighthouse? I can pack a picnic."

"That sounds like fun. I'll bring a blanket and the beverages."

"Just remember," Ivy reminded him, "no alcohol on the beach."

"Not a problem. Pop it is! Can I pick you up?"

"Sure," and as she gave him her address, the first thought through Ivy's mind was that she had a lot of cleaning to do. Gentleman that he was, he was sure to come to the door.

Saturday turned out to be one of those idyllic days – a clear blue sky, with virtually no wind, and just enough warmth to encourage a person to remove her lightweight jacket. Ivy had spent all of Friday evening, pushing and shoving things in closets and drawers, then she ran a dust cloth over all surfaces, and lastly did a well needed vacuuming. The place hadn't looked this good in months.

She dressed in jeans, a soft yellow tee, and a navy hoodie. Her light brown hair was tied up in a ponytail, the sun-kissed streaks swaying as she moved. Before she was completely ready, the doorbell rang. She ran to the bathroom and made a quick swipe of pink lipstick over her full lips, then quickly grabbed the door. She paused a moment to catch her breath before opening it. She was nervous and excited at the same time, almost afraid that Fox would do something wrong today, to shatter the idea of the man she thought him to be.

But when she pulled open the door, she was taken aback at the image before her. He was hatless today, but with his hair slicked straight back, he was the picture of perfection. The slim jeans and snug tee shirt showed off his slender physique. The dimple in his chin seemed more pronounced today, because he was not quite as clean shaven as he had been in the past. The dark stubble only emphasized his manliness. He handed her daisies wrapped in green florist tissue paper. Standing before her was the epitome of a self-assured man, and everything she had ever dreamed of.

"Am I too early?" he asked.

"What? Uh, no, not at all." 'Where are my manners,' she thought. She was aware she was staring at the man, but it was impossible to take her eyes off of him. "Would you care to step in for a moment? I have to grab my purse, and I was just about to fill Percy's bowls."

"Percy?"

"Yes, my cat. He's shy, so you won't see him right away. Do you like cats?" This was the test. No cats – no man.

"I love cats. Actually, I love all animals, but cats and dogs especially."

"Not allergic, then?"

"Not a bit."

Ivy breathed a sigh of relief. He had passed. "Wonderful. Okay, just a minute, then. I've already put food in his bowl. I'll get him some fresh water, and we can be on our way."

When they were ready to go, he closed the door for her, and placed his hand on the small of her back as they walked to the car. Ivy sighed with pleasure. She heard the door down the hallway quietly close; most likely Nancy had been peeking out.

≈

Fox had the top down on his bright red Mazda.

"Nice ride," said Ivy. "This isn't the same car you were driving before."

Fox's face lit up like a school boy, as he talked about his car. "No, the 4-wheel drive is for winter. This is my summer baby. She only comes out after the salt is off the road. It's a 2012 Mazda MX-5 Miata, Special Edition. Isn't she something?" He caressed the fender like a man in love.

Ivy laughed. "You talk about it as if it's a person – a female."

"Sure, don't all men do that? She purrs like a kitten. She's a 4-cylinder, 6 speed, with 167 horsepower at 7000 rpm's."

"Well, that actually means nothing to me, but it — she is pretty. What's her name?"

"How did you know I named her?"

"My dad always named his cars. So spill — what's her name?"

"Ruby." Fox was so busy looking over his beauty on wheels as he spoke, that he had not seen the look of shock on Ivy's face.

"R — Ruby?"

"Sure, you know, because she's red, I guess."

Visibly shaken, and wondering if this was some kind of sign, Ivy covered by saying, "Well, let's take *her* for a ride."

Fox took her hand while she lowered herself into the seat, and then ran around to his side of the car and got in, closing the door with a solid thump.

"Would you like a scarf for your hair?"

"Hmm, do you offer scarves to all of your ladies?" she teased.

"Actually, I do. I have three sisters and five nieces."

"Big family – and yes, thank you, I'll take a scarf."

As Fox leaned over Ivy's lap, enjoying the closeness as he did so, he reached into the glovebox. "Here you go," he said seductively, not removing his body from her lap. The car was small, and as he slowly sat up, Ivy was aware of how close his face was to hers. Her heart was racing. She could see deep into his eyes, a place where a girl could get lost. She could smell his soap and shampoo blended into one, a manly smell that was so intoxicating that she could barely breathe. She waited for the kiss she found herself longing for, but instead he pulled back, never taking his eyes off of hers.

When Ivy looked at the scarf, she saw a beautiful, gold, silk pashmina. It was luxurious and felt very sexy slipping through her fingers. "It's lovely. And it's brand new."

"How do you know?" His eyes crinkled when he smiled.

"There's still a price tag hanging on it."

"Oops, sorry, let me remove that."

"So, no one else has ever worn it?" asked Ivy softly.

"Not a sister, niece, and anyone else. I actually bought it on the day after I met you." His voice was low and husky.

"You did?"

"Yes, the day you tangled me up in your red scarf. When you arrived at the diner, you were wearing a swirly orange pashmina – and I only know what they are called because of the females in my family," he chuckled.

Ivy smiled, pleased that he would remember what she had been wearing. As she fashioned the scarf on her head, he continued.

"I had not been able to find the right gift for my niece, Abby – she's a sophomore in college – so I went shopping again the next day. When I saw this, the color reminded me of the flecks in your eyes and the streaks in your hair." He reached out and gently tucked in an errant strand. Ivy shivered at the intimacy.

There was an awkward pause, until she came out of her romantic fog. Fox started to lean in for a kiss, she was sure of it, but she had already started to talk. She

246

said lightly, "Well, we'd better get going, before the Michigan weather does an about face on us."

They laughed easily together, and as he started the engine to a roar, and shifted into gear, Ivy was thrown back into her seat, truly happy for the first time in months, as the little red car named Ruby took her to Wabaningo.

Chapter Twenty-three

The afternoon couldn't have been more perfect. The cumulus clouds looking like large puffs of cotton against the azure sky added to the magical day. Fox and Ivy stopped at the White River Lighthouse and Museum, and took the tour to the top of the light itself where they discovered a gorgeous view of the White Lake channel and Lake Michigan. Fox had his arm around her in a very intimate manner; at such a height, Ivy felt like she was in Heaven.

"This is perfect, Fox. Thank you. I've never been to the top before," Ivy said as she scanned the horizon.

"Me, either. I'm so glad I could be the one to share this experience with you for the first time," he said softly. As Ivy turned from the blue of the water to the deep brown of his eyes, she felt herself slowly leaning closer to him – or was it Fox who was coming toward her? Whatever had caused the momentum to begin no longer mattered.

As Fox stared at the beauty before him, all he wanted was to taste her lips, smell her hair, and feel her body as it formed to his. He needed to know what having Ivy all to himself meant. He pulled her in gently and placed his lips on hers. It was everything he had thought it would be – as sweet as honey. He was afraid to come on too strong in these close quarters when they were completely alone, but at the same time that is all he really wanted. He brought her in close. Their heights were a perfect match, and he was pleased to feel that the contour of her body fit in all the right places. It was like pulling on a pair of soft leather gloves – sensual and warm.

Ivy felt something she had never felt with a man before. She had kissed her share of frogs, but this time she never wanted the kiss to end. She couldn't breathe and at the same time she felt as if she were floating on air. Her heart was racing, her toes tingled, and her stomach did flip-flops, while other sensations surfaced she didn't even know existed. No man had ever caused her to feel emotions to this extent. If they had not been in a public place, she would have let him do anything he wanted with her. She needed to gain control before it was too late. And just as she was thinking that thought, he pulled away, as if he had read her mind. The loss of his lips on hers left her empty. She wanted to fill up again and again. Ivy leaned in for more, as Fox looked at her in surprise. He would never have guessed that this shy and conservative woman had this much passion in her. He was pleased -- very pleased. He smiled and offered his mouth to her once more, but a baby's squeal and children's heavy footsteps on the stairs could be heard as the parents called out warnings to their brood. Ivy and Fox stepped aside as the young viewers came bounding up. The new couple made their descent down, laughing all the way, at almost getting caught.

"Did you enjoy yourselves up there?" called out the docent.

"Yes, I did, very much. Thank you," responded Fox.

Ivy blushed, and the older man chuckled, knowing full well what had most likely taken place.

"Where to now?" asked Ivy.

"Feel like walking? We can take the walk along the channel a little way."

"That sounds nice."

They walked hand in hand, talking, teasing, and laughing the way long-time lovers do. Ivy was so enjoying herself that she was hoping the day would never end. "Wait. What about the car? We left our picnic lunch back at the lighthouse parking lot."

"Oops, you're right. How about we walk a little farther, then go back to the car and drive our picnic around to the beach."

"Perfect."

They continued on the boardwalk until they could go no further, because turning around would mean the day was coming closer to an end and the thought of that happening was almost unbearable. And suddenly, true to form to the unpredictable Michigan weather, dark clouds began to roll in and the wind picked up its strength causing the waves to crash more forcefully against the breaker. As small raindrops began to fall, they were forced to turn around, picking up their pace, and finally as the deluge let loose, they ran, soaked to the skin, laughing all the way.

Fox had put up the top of the small convertible before they walked away from the car, mostly for security purposes. They were happy with the dry seats and the warmth that came forth once the heater took effect.

"Well, that's a turn of events, isn't it?" he said.

"That's living along the lakeshore for you. You've heard it before, but it is so true. 'If you don't like the weather, just wait a minute.'"

Fox thought a moment. "What now? We're both drenched."

Ivy was so comfortable with Fox at this point that she had no problem saying, "We could always go back to my place, dry off, and have our picnic lunch there."

It was more than Fox could have hoped for. More time with Ivy was all he wanted, but being in close quarters with her in her apartment with no one to interrupt them would take all of the restraint he could muster. She was a grown woman, but she was fragile, and it was most likely too soon in their relationship for her to want him as much as he wanted her.

Ivy hoped she had done the right thing, suggesting they go back to her place. She was a grown woman, after all, but could she trust him? Or more to the point, could she trust herself?

By the time Fox and Ivy had arrived at her apartment, the rain had settled into a dreary drizzle that promised to last a while. Fox held an umbrella over Ivy's head, as she reached in the trunk for her picnic basket. Ivy led the way to her front door, splashing water from a puddle onto the pant legs of her jeans.

Once they were inside, they realized how cold and wet they were. Ivy ran to get some towels to dry their hair and wipe off as much excess moisture they could, then she clicked the button for the gas flame in her fireplace, the one extravagance to this apartment and the main reason she had moved in here. She love watching Fox towel dry his hair. He looked so different when it wasn't perfectly combed, almost like a little boy. After removing his shirt so she could hang it over a chair to dry, he stood, bare-chested, by the flames of the fireplace. As he wiped down his arms, she was surprised at the strength that had been concealed under his clothing. Muscles moved and rippled on his forearms and biceps in the flickering light. His shoulders were broad, tapering to his slender waist. He seemed completely unaware of the effect he was having on her. After drying off the best he could, he loosely slung the towel around his neck; it pointed downward, accenting the position of his jeans, which sat precariously low on his hips.

While Ivy studied the view in front of her, she removed her own dripping-wet sweatshirt, and was in the process of taking out her ponytail holder. It had gotten tangled in her wet hair, and was refusing to move. Fox saw her struggle and slowly stepped forward to offer his assistance.

"Here, let me help you with that." He reached out to touch her hair, but first his hand settled on the side of her head, stroking down to her cheek, and caressing gently as his thumb traveled over her jawline. "Turn around," he said huskily.

Ivy did what she was told, knowing she would not deny him anything. He carefully tugged until the tangled mess released, ran his fingers through her hair as if they were a comb, then he cupped her head and kissed the side of her neck. Ivy leaned back towards him, as he slipped his arms around her waist. She could feel the heat of his bare chest through her wet shirt. They stood quietly for a few moments, taking in the joy of being together.

"You're pretty good at getting out tangles," Ivy sighed.

"I've got sisters, remember?" he whispered in her ear. He turned her around to face him, saying, "But you're nothing like one of my sisters." And with a hand on each side of her face, he kissed her full on the mouth. Ivy could have stayed in his arms for the rest of the day, but it was Fox who pulled away first.

Fox studied Ivy's face a moment, as if making a decision on his next move. Once he had his emotions in check, he said lightly, "Now, how about getting something to eat? I'm starving." He laughed at the little girl disappointment on her face. He thought he should have just taken her to the bedroom right then, but he wanted her to be sure. He had no intention of forcing her to do anything. Fox had known from the moment that he first spotted her in the grocery aisle that this was the woman he wanted, and now he was positive he had fallen deeply for this beautiful, sexy creature standing in front of him with her tee shirt so damp that he could see right through it. But he was not about to push her; he would let her make the first move.

Embarrassed by her desires, Ivy stumbled to correct her awkwardness. "Oh, you're right. Food. Yes, the reason why we came here. Uh – yes – uh, are you warm enough? Can I get you another towel to wrap around your – uh – shoulders? Or a blanket? Um -- I should put on another top. Do you need anything?"

"I'm fine. Or I will be as soon as I get something to eat. Fuel for the body, you know. What's to eat?"

And, suddenly, they were like a happy couple who had been together for a long time. Fox pulled out the sub sandwiches that Ivy had picked up at the deli, as Ivy got out the paper plates and napkins. "Oh," said Ivy, "we left the beverages in the car. I have wine, if you drink wine, that is. Sorry, no beer; I don't drink it."

"Wine is fine with me," said Fox enjoying their easy exchange. It was so nice to be with a woman and not have to wonder what to say or do to make the conversation flow.

"Let's sit over there," Ivy pointed. "It'll be more like a picnic." They carried their lunch to the rug on the floor in front of the fireplace. Ivy propped up pillows behind their back against the couch. "Tell, me more about yourself," she said as they fussed with their seating arrangement.

Fox rambled on about his days as a little kid, to his college exploits. Ivy loved to hear the sound of his voice. It had been so long since she had allowed a man to come to her place. The wine lulled her into a warm feeling of security. She watched his face as he talked, staring deeply into his eyes, so entranced, she sometimes forgot to listen to the words. He was open, holding nothing back, even telling some of his most embarrassing stories. Then he began to talk about his interest in history.

"History? What kind of history? Like the Civil War or the American Revolution?" This was a new side to him. She was eager to hear about it.

"Now, don't laugh. But I'm a bit of a fanatic when it comes to Prohibition."

Ivy gasped. Fox took it as surprise that anyone would be fascinated in that mob infested era. "I know, weird, right?"

Ivy glanced at the photo of Ruby and Sal sitting on her desk. What did he know? What could he possibly know about her GG? Nothing. She had never mentioned anything about her grandmother's past. She smiled to herself over her paranoia; it was sheer coincidence, that's all. "Why Prohibition?"

His face lit up as he told her about growing up on the east side of the state where The Purple Gang had all the control over the Canada bootlegging operation. He recounted how they had struck a deal with Al Capone, so that each gang controlled half of the state of Michigan, but that they needed each other to survive.

"Have you ever heard of blind pigs?"

"I can't say that I have." Ivy laughed at his enthusiasm.

"That's what they called any place that sold illegal alcohol. Because of the closeness to Canada, Detroit alone had over 25,000 of them at one time."

"How did the alcohol come into the state?"

"Sometimes women smuggled bottles under their dresses, strapped to their legs. That's where the term bootlegging came from. There's one area in Michigan where Canada is literally only one mile away, across the Detroit River. During the summer, small boats were running at night. One famous operation was a cable that ran under the river which connected to an underwater boat; can you believe that? In the winter, they actually figured out how to make sleds loaded with booze that they would pull across. They were ingenious."

Ivy was very interested in this lesson. She could see now that he had no knowledge of her family's involvement. "When did Prohibition end?"

"It actually ended in 1933, when the federal government finally repealed it, but many counties and individual cities held on to it for a long time. I just recently found out that a town called Hudsonville in Ottawa County was dry until 2007."

"2007? Are you kidding me?"

"No, and even when they finally passed the right to sell liquor, they still banned sales on Sunday."

"Speaking of alcohol --

She stretched across his body for the almost empty bottle. Her closeness took his breath away; he shivered with anticipation. He needed her now, but he could wait. He decided to change the subject when he realized he had done all of the talking. "Enough about me. Now it's your turn."

"Well, there's not much to tell," said Ivy. "I was born and raised in this area, moved away for a bit, and came back when my grandmothers needed me. I've told you that already. You already know that I come from a dysfunctional family."

"Most people do."

"Well, it's only dysfunctional as far as my father goes; otherwise I was raised by three loving women, and all of them are gone now."

"Sorry, I didn't mean to bring up your loss."

Ivy thought a moment, and knew what she was about to say was true. "That's okay. It doesn't hurt so much anymore. My life has been much fuller lately."

"It has?" he asked, hoping it was because of him.

"Yes, I think writing the story about GG helped a lot." She saw his disappointment and added, "And I met this pretty great guy."

"You did?" he teased. "Could this great guy be me, by any chance?"

"Yes, as a matter of fact, it could be. It is." It was at that moment that Ivy knew no matter how quickly this had happened, she had fallen head over heels in love with Fox. They seemed destined for one another. She had never in all of her life felt this way before. Once, when she had asked her Nana how she would know when she was in love, Nana's answer was, 'if you have to ask yourself if you are, then you're not.' Today, looking at the curl that had fallen over Fox's brow, Ivy did not question it one bit; she had never been more certain of anything in her entire life. She flashed Fox a smile, while she placed her plate on the side table, seductively sending him a signal all men recognized.

Fox put down his wine glass and happily took the woman he loved in his arms. It was the invitation he had been waiting for the whole day.

Their passion for each other was electric. They spent the rest of the day and evening wrapped up in blankets and then unwrapped again, as the rain continued its steady patter outside the window. They moved from the floor, to the bed, and after getting up for another bottle of wine, they moved back to the floor in front of the fire once again, and then later to the couch, where they snuggled up together, naked, and completely uninhibited. They continued talking, learning more about each other every hour that they weren't engaged in making love. Ivy couldn't get enough of him. He knew he would never get enough of her.

Percy finally came out of hiding when it was time for food, and he stayed with them, curled up on their blankets, next to the fire. Ivy enjoyed watching Fox stroke her cat, as it purred its acceptance of him.

And finally the hour came when Fox said he must go. He had an early appointment tomorrow. "On Sunday?" Ivy said, more than a little disappointed.

"Well, it's not really an appointment, but I have to complete my job, since I goofed off today. Something distracted me," he teased. "I'm scheduled to go back home late in the afternoon."

"Would you like to come for dinner before you leave?" Ivy was hoping he wanted to see her again; she would love to keep him with her as long as possible.

He laughed, and tugged her to him once again, "I think that can be arranged." After a few more minutes of silence as the lovers said their goodbyes, Fox rose, pulled on his clothing, grinning all the while he yanked on his socks. He brushed his hands over his hair, but the lock fell forward again, anyway. Ivy reached out to touch it, coaxing it back into place. "The reason I use gel," he chuckled.

"It's very sexy," she said softly, as she kissed him gently.

"Now, Ivy, I have to go. I need to get a shower and some clean clothes. What time do you want me back tomorrow?"

"Any time after two is fine; after that I'll be here all afternoon waiting for you. Text before you come, and I'll unlock the door. I could be wearing something you'll want to see," she giggled seductively.

"Hmm, I can't imagine anything more beautiful than what I saw tonight, but I'll be here. Maybe we can have fun removing it." They kissed again, and then Ivy closed the door. She leaned her back against it, closed her eyes, and a single tear of joy coursed its way down her cheek in a zigzag pattern.

Chapter Twenty-four

After Fox left, Ivy had the best sleep in her life, with what was left of the night. She stretched languorously, as she tried to imprint in her brain every detail of the night before. Could this man be any more perfect for her? It was as if GG herself had picked him out. With the thought of GG, Ivy realized that she had a mission to accomplish before Fox returned later this afternoon. She quickly jumped out of bed, took a hot shower, and got dressed for her errand.

In her rush to feed Percy, and get out the door before too much more of the day disappeared, she knocked over the framed picture of Ruby and Sal when she was reaching for her purse. As she righted it, she was disappointed to see that she had cracked the glass. "Shoot. Well, it's just the glass; the frame's still okay.

I'll fix it later," she said to herself, but then she thought about Percy getting into trouble, as he usually did. He sometimes walked all over the desk, taking naps on top of her bills. She held the frame over the garbage can, as she carefully removed the picture and then disposed of the glass.

Holding the photo in her hand, she studied Ruby and Sal one more time. They were so much in love. Did she feel the same way about Fox? The passion was certainly there. But would it last over a lifetime as it had for Ruby? Was the reason she was so attracted to Fox because of the way he wore his hat, or the way he looked at her with the same cocky self-assurance as Sal? Was it real love that she felt, or just a romantic idea of having what her great-grandmother had had? Fox certainly did resemble Sal, in that old world Italian-American way. For some odd reason, Ivy turned over the picture. It had never been out of the frame before, so she was shocked to see a series of letters and numbers on the back. It said, 'R31, L29, R15, L22'. Ivy stared for a long time, her hands quivering on the photo. It was a combination. THE combination. She picked up the phone and called Nancy.

"Nance, did I wake you?"

"Not really. Matt is home for the weekend, so we're making the most of it, if you know what I mean," she giggled. Ivy could hear a muffled voice.

"Oh, sorry, tell him I apologize. You shouldn't have answered the phone."

"No, we – well, I was about to get up to make coffee, anyway. What's up?"

"I saw you peek out the door when Fox came for me yesterday. What did you think?"

"He's pretty hot, I'll grant you that. And I think he was probably there late into the night; am I right?"

"Yes, he was. Oh, Nancy, he's so perfect, I can't believe it. It's like we've always been together, and yet it's so exciting because it's all so new."

"Well, someone is on cloud nine."

Ivy could hear the water running as Nancy filled her coffee pot. "I so am! I'm up so high it scares me."

"Just go with it. Enjoy it. It's been a long time since you've been interested in anyone. Are you seeing him again soon?"

"Actually, he's coming back this afternoon. I'm running out to the cottage to finish up out there. I got a notice from my attorney that my time is up. I have to vacate the rest of the stuff this week. The appraiser will be there any day, and then it's going to auction."

"I'm so sorry. I wish there was something you could do. Have you heard back from the bank on a possible mortgage, so you could bid on it yourself?"

"I did, but I'm not approved for as much as I thought I would be, and without a down payment of my own, they won't lend me anything. So I have to face the fact that the cottage will no longer be in the family."

"What about your dad?"

"I'd never ask him for a dime. He wasn't interested in GG when she was alive, why would he care now. He obviously doesn't give a hoot about me. Anyway, I had another reason for calling. I discovered something, and I was so excited that I had to tell you."

"What? Something about Fox?"

"No, but you'll never believe it. I found the combination to the safe." Ivy held her breath waiting for the squeal she knew would come. And it did.

She heard Matt say, "What's going on?"

"Nothing, hon. It's just Ivy. I'll have our coffee in a minute."

Nancy turned her attention back to the phone. "Now tell me. Where? And what are you going to do about it?"

"It was there all along. On the back of the picture of Ruby and Sal. I'm going to look for the money in the boathouse today, and I'll have to force myself to go down into the cellar. I was going to ask you to go with me, but I know how precious your time is with your fireman."

"Sorry, Ivy. I would have loved to go on this adventure with you."

"No problem. I'll fill you in later. After Fox leaves, of course."

"Okay, bye, hon. Be careful. Both at the cottage and in love," she laughed.

$$\approx$$

Ivy drove straight out to Wabaningo, heart racing all the way. She had entered the safe combination numbers on her phone in the notes folder. When she arrived, one quick look at the sky alerted her to another incoming storm. So as anxious as she was to get to the safe, she decided to head to the boathouse first, before she got rained on as she had yesterday. Remembering Fox and herself wet and cold, and then warming each other skin to skin, brought a blush to the surface. She was really looking forward to this afternoon and what was to come.

Grabbing her lantern and the backpack, heavy with flashlights and a trowel, she trudged toward the lake and the dock, through the wet grass and mud, glad she had remembered to wear her muck boots. She had the key to the boathouse on her keychain, and after rattling the rusty lock for a few seconds, she finally gained entry. It was dark and damp. The smell of dusty canvas tarps, old oil, and a slight odor of fish assaulted her nostrils, but strangely enough to her, it was good scent, familiar and comforting, bringing back memories of happy days when she was free to swim and fish at will.

The LED lantern she had brought lit up the small building just fine, but created eerie shadows in the corners. The electricity had long ago been turned off, most likely from lack of payment to the power company. She felt terrible that she had not thought about GG's house and how it would need upkeep. And now because of her lack of attention, the house was going back to the City for back taxes. But as her attorney pointed out, even if she had paid the taxes, the State would still take the house to recoup as much of the Medicaid payments as possible. And there was nothing she could do about it.

Ivy walked around looking at the various odds and ends that had been stored there. Nothing much of value that she could tell. Maybe the antique oars and wicker fishing creel would be of interest to a collector. And she had heard that some lures could bring in money, also. She set those aside to take to an antique shop later. Then she spotted a rusty red tool box pushed to the back of the work bench. She lifted the lid and found some wrenches and screwdrivers of various sizes, screws, nails, and string. As she pulled up the handle on the shelf insert, she sucked in her breath at the yellowed, dirty envelope, sitting underneath. It looked fat. Could it be what she thought it was? Is it possible that some of the hidden money was still in existence? She lifted the envelope, surprised at the weight of it. Ivy almost passed out when she discovered a fat bundle of bills – a variety of denominations, but as she flipped through it, she saw many 50s and 100s. She heard a twig snap so she quickly stuffed it in her backpack. She decided it was best to move as fast as possible; she would count it later.

She waited for what seemed an eternity, and when she could detect no movement outside, she threw back an old tarp that was on top of a few boxes and crates. Hadn't Ruby said there was some money buried under a tarp? Ivy had not thought to carry her shovel with her, but there was one leaning against a wall, as if waiting for this particular job. She pushed and shoved the boxes out of the way, working as if her life depended on it, in case someone really did show up. But then, why would they? No one but Nancy knew she was here. She began to dig in the wet ground, unsure of where to start exactly. It took her a half hour of digging, as she made her circle larger and deeper with each shovelful, but finally she hit a satisfying clunk. The lantern was on the lowest setting and she was unable to see as well as she wanted, so she turned up the brightness. Holding it over the hole, she could see something that was blue metal. Eager to get to it, she dropped to her knees and began digging with her trowel and finally with her hands, until she was able to pull the toolbox from the earth; it was slightly larger than the one she had already opened. She tugged and pulled at the stubborn latch in order to yank it loose, and then with one more forceful jerk, it released

With her hands muddy, her knees soaked through, and her face filthy with sweat and dirt, she let out a quiet whistle as she stared at the contents. It was full to the brim with one hundred dollar bills. When she came to her senses, she began to stuff the money into the backpack with the previous bundle. She buried the hole, pulled back the tarp, and collected everything she had set aside with her. Then she locked the door to the boathouse, and walked as fast as she could to her car. Glancing around, she tossed the bag, heavy with bills, in the trunk. She really didn't want to separate herself from the money, but she had no choice. There was more to do. Now, she felt as if there was a real possibility of finding GG's ruby and diamond necklace, and like it or not, she needed to go down that cellar.

Chapter Twenty-five

One thing few people knew about Ivy was that she was frightened of the dark. Going down the cellar with no one else around was one of the scariest things she could imagine. After pushing the table aside, and lifting the rug, the basement door was exposed. It squeaked as she pulled it open. Ivy got down on her knees, turned on her flashlight, and then aiming the beam down below, she slowly put her head in the opening. The room was surprisingly small and round. She shined the light slowly around as much of the area as she could reach, and when she was assured there was nothing to be afraid of, she lowered herself down the ladder-steps, taking her lantern with her.

As soon as Ivy's feet hit the ground, she realized her mistake in not turning the lantern on up above. It was difficult to twist it on with the lantern in one hand and the flashlight in the other. She laid the flashlight down, then squatted and positioned herself in its beam. Once she found the knob on the top, thanking God for battery-operated lanterns, she turned the light to its highest setting. Now that she could see, she felt a lot better, and her heart rate began to slow to a steady beat. She kept reminding herself that no one knew she was here, and no one could possibly know about her discovery in the boathouse.

If the area she stood in had been a square room, it would have been about a ten-foot square. Shelves lined the walls with old canning equipment, mason jars, and a lot of cobwebs. Ivy gasped when she saw what she had been hoping to find. There it was, back in the farthest corner -- large, black, and very dusty. She ran her hands over the front in order to reveal the letters, and when she did she exposed the ornate gold trim with lettering that said 'Trumball Safe and Vault, Chicago Illinois, est. 1898.' It was on large caster wheels, but was obviously so heavy there was no way any one person could have moved it around a room. Once it was placed in its position, in the 1930s, it had stayed to rest.

Ivy looked over the walls, wondering how it had been brought down here. For the most part, the area was what was called a Michigan basement, meaning the walls were made of large rocks, most likely found on the property, and stacked closely together, to hold back the earth. It was solid and had done a good job of holding back the dampness of the high water table. Ivy sighed with anticipation, knowing it was time to do what she had come for. She took out her phone and opened her notes folder to the page she had listed as simply, 'numbers.' She took a deep breath, and with a shaky hand she first gave the tumbler dial a spin, to make sure it was free of any numbers from the previous opening. She turned right to 31, then went left to 29, then right again to 15, then back left to 22. She stopped, at that point, with quivering hands, afraid to breathe, then she pulled the handle with a downward yank. It released easily with a soft clink. Ivy slowly pulled open the heavy door, and stood quietly staring. Nothing. It was empty.

Tears filled her eyes as she said, with a weak and disappointed voice, "I'm so sorry, Ruby. I tried."

Suddenly she heard footsteps overhead. 'Who could possibly be here?' she wondered. She stayed perfectly still wondering what to do. Her first instinct was to slam the safe closed, but what good would that do? There was nothing to hide.

"Hello?" called a male voice.

Wondering whether she should make her presence known, she stood quietly for a moment, trying to sort it out. She was down in a cellar with no way out, and she was all alone.

"Helloooo. Is anyone here? I saw a car outside. Anyone?"

With the longer sentences, Ivy was shocked to recognize Fox's voice.

"Fox?" She moved toward the ladder, but before she was able to come up, he popped his head in the opening.

"Ivy? What are you doing here?"

"I think the question is: what are *you* doing here?" she laughed. "Are you stalking me?" she asked teasingly. She began her ascent to the main floor. He was there to offer her a hand as she placed her foot in her great-grandmother's kitchen, happy to be above ground once more. She leaned in for a kiss. "Mmmm. It's good to see you."

"I really don't understand," said Fox with a puzzled look on his face. "I'm working."

"What? What do you mean working?" He was trying to pull her into his arms, but she resisted, needing to hear his explanation; her joy had just crumbled at finding him here in her grandmother's house. She stepped back, trying to sort it out, furthering his confusion.

"I told you, I do appraisals for the State. I'm here to appraise this house."

"You never said you worked for the State of Michigan. I thought you worked for a real estate company." Ivy was highly irritated now, and Fox couldn't figure out why.

"I do, but we contract out to the State. I appraise houses for the Medicaid Retrieval program."

"Medicaid? You're the one who is taking my GG's house away from me?"

"What? No, Ivy," he pleaded, "I didn't know this was your grandmother's house. You never told me her name. And besides, I just estimate the value before it goes to auction, so we have an approximate starting point for the bids." He could see the pain in her eyes. "Ivy, please, it's just my job. I had no idea –

"You had no idea? No idea? Tell the truth! You knew all along who my GG was. You were just trying to get information." Panic was setting in now. She had a bag full of money in the trunk of her car, and she had no idea who knew it had been hidden on the property. Her grandmother had been part of a bootlegging operation that had brought in thousands and thousands of dollars of illegal money.

"What in the world are you talking about?" Fox had done something terribly wrong, but he could not for the life of him figure it out.

Ivy was sobbing now. Her hair was a mess, her face was dirt-streaked, her jeans were muddy, and Fox thought she had never looked more enticing. He wanted nothing more than to hold her and comfort her, and calm her down. He reached for her once again, and she slapped him hard on the face. She was completely out of control, now, sobbing so hard he could hardly make out what she was saying.

"You used me. You used me to your advantage. I thought we had something special, but it was all a lie!" she yelled.

Fox was so shocked at what she had said that he did not even feel the slap, even though it was turning his cheek a bright crimson red. He stood in silence hoping her tirade would end, so he could talk to her rationally and get to the bottom of this.

"I'm sorry, Ivy, but I still don't get it. All I do is walk through houses and turn in a report. I do nothing else."

"And if you happen to hear of one that fits your interest in Prohibition, you do what? Steal things for your collection? Look for treasure? What is it you want here, Fox?" she snarled. Ivy did not ever remember being this angry at someone, other than her father, in her entire life. And just like her father and the ex-boyfriend she had left behind, Fox had let her down, but this time the betrayal was different, because she had fallen in love. She had trusted him. She had been ready to give him her heart unconditionally.

"Go ahead, look down below. The safe is open now, if that's what you came for. Help yourself. There's nothing there."

"Safe? What safe? I don't know anything about a safe. This is the first time I've ever been in this house."

"You know you're looking for GG's necklace, and so do I, so come clean. Stop trying to cover your tracks."

"Oh, for Pete's sake. How else can I convince you that I don't know anything about a necklace, a safe, or your great-grandmother's house? You never mentioned a necklace. And think about it, when I told you about my hobby and interest in the 1920s and '30s, you never mentioned her, then, either. You've made a big mistake, here."

"My mistake was falling in love with you. Now move out of the way." She gave him a shove as she moved past him.

"You love me?" For a second his face lit up, but it was immediately followed by his utter devastation as she slammed the door.

Even though the heavy rain clouds had moved in bringing huge drops which were beating down on her, she walked with a steady pace, her back to the house. She would not let him see her crumpled face as she cried over him. She was done. She'd been hurt too many times in her life and this was the last straw. She had left her flashlight and lantern behind, but that was okay, because she would never return to her beloved GG's cottage again. He could have it all. Ruby's necklace was gone forever, along with the love of her life.

Chapter Twenty-six

The first thing Ivy did when she arrived back in her apartment was take a shower. She scrubbed away the mud and grime of the day right along with her emotions, and she watched with satisfaction as they swirled down the drain. It was easier to cry in the shower where not even Percy could hear her sobs. The tears blended in with the cascading drops that she had set to the highest heat that she could bear; here the salt water tears would blend with the conditioned water and she would not need to wipe them away, using wadded up tissues, and feeling like a fool. But once she was standing in front of the mirror, her face puffy and her eyes red-rimmed, she had to face the truth. She had been duped. Somehow, Fox had discovered that Ruby was part of the bootlegging ring, and he most likely suspected there could be a treasure of some kind in that house. As she towel-dried her hair, she went over and over her meetings with him. He had said that he had seen her before the time they first met in the parking lot in front of her work. He mentioned he had noticed her at the nursing home. Had he been there, prying information from Ruby, even before she, herself, had been told the story? Had he seen her in the halls while she was visiting and decided then and there to take advantage of that situation? He certainly would have been aware of what houses would be on the list for the State recovery program. Putting it all together with the fact that he had told her he enjoyed history and liked to chase down stories about it, she now wondered how she could have been so blind.

Ivy's phone began to vibrate on the counter next to her. As soon as she saw Fox's number show up, she tapped the red dot. She would never talk to him again. The ringtone sounded again and again, until she turned off the ringer. But then the window began to light up with text messages, and still, she refused to answer him.

"Are we still on for this afternoon?"

"Ivy, please, let me explain."

"I love you, please give me another chance."

"We need to talk. You totally misunderstood."

"Let me explain myself."

And then finally the messages stopped coming in. Ivy felt so lost she didn't know what to do. The apartment was empty without him. She needed his arms around her. He was the one she wanted to comfort her; she ached for him, but he was the cause of the misery. She did the only thing she could think of. She called her best friend.

"Nancy? Can we talk?" He voice cracked as she tried to keep her emotions in check.

Nancy could tell instantly that her friend needed her. "Sure, of course, I'll be over in a few minutes. Matt was just leaving for his three-day shift at the firehouse. I'll have all the time you need for the rest of the day."

When Nancy took one look at her friend's face, it was obvious that this was something serious. Nancy was worried that her friend had slipped into a depression again; she hoped she could help in some way.

"What's going on?"

"I feel like such a fool." Ivy tried her best to hold back the flow of tears, but they continued to leak out and run silently down her face.

"Let's sit on the couch, and you can tell me all about it. I thought you were going to the cottage. What happened?

Ivy told her every detail she could remember, even trusting her friend with the fact that she had found money.

"Money? Really? How much? Like a lot?"

"Yes, a lot. I haven't even counted it yet, but probably thousands."

"Thousands? But what does all of this have to do with Fox?"

Then Ivy went on to tell the rest of the story and how deceived she had felt.

"Are you sure he knew that the cottage belonged to your grandmother?"

"He said he didn't, and he did look surprised at seeing me there, but most likely that was because he thought he would be alone, while he conducted his search. I don't trust him one bit. And to make matters worse, I had already opened the safe. He found me in the cellar. So now he knows I was looking for something."

"You opened it? Was anything inside? Any sign of the necklace?"

"No, it was empty. I had to give up. The house will go up for auction now, and there's no chance I can go back. Besides I wouldn't, anyway, if I thought Fox was in town. I'm sure the necklace is gone. Maybe Sal never hid it, maybe he sold it and that's where all of the money came from."

The phone lit up again, as Fox tried one more time to reach Ivy. Nancy picked it up, intending to hand it to Ivy, but Ivy shook her head no.

"Maybe you should give him a chance to explain. Is it possible you did misunderstand, as he said?"

"No, I didn't. I can see the whole thing clearly. Our meeting was all a big setup. He was looking for something all right, and he got more than he expected. I gave him more of myself than I have ever given anyone in my life. I'll never forgive him. Especially for last night. He can have the house and all that's in it."

"Ivy, this is getting out of control. Fox doesn't get the house. It has to be sold at auction for the State to recover their money. You know that. How much do you think the house will go for?"

"More than I have. I tried to get a loan and the bank turned me down."

Nancy grinned. "But didn't you just tell me you had money now? Let's count it and see. Maybe we can work something out."

Nancy was shocked when she saw the haul Ivy had in the backpack. "Nancy, if anyone ever finds out about this money, I'll know you told. No one else on Earth knows about it – well, I thought that until earlier today. Somehow he found out, I'm sure of it."

"Well, I ain't no stool pigeon," she laughed, pretending to flick a cigar. "And forget about Fox; he's of no concern to us right now. Let's count this out."

They sorted the bills into piles according to their denominations. When they had completed that task, they were shocked to see the amount and height of the green stacks.

"Money sure has a distinctive smell when it's all in a pile like this, doesn't it?" said Ivy. "I've never seen anything like this before."

"I was a bank teller for a while, not long because I didn't like the responsibility of balancing out every night. If you were missing anything, even a dime, it came out of your pay. I'm a very honest person, but for some reason, I was always short. It was not the job for me, but I did get a chance to see an armored car delivery, once. When the bags were emptied on a cart, it held one million dollars. It took up way more space than I had expected it to. But I never thought I would see this much money on a kitchen table."

"Let's get a calculator and start counting," said Ivy, temporarily forgetting about the man who had caused her misery.

After counting the piles twice, they were satisfied with the tally. Nancy said, "I think this calls for wine!"

"Fifty thousand dollars? Are you sure?" Ivy was in shock. "How much was that back in the '30s?"

Nancy bit her lip trying to figure out how they could find out. "Grab your laptop. You can find out anything there."

The two women sat on the couch side by side. Ivy typed in '1930s money compared to today.'

"Yes," yelled out Ivy. "Look at this site. It says that one dollar in 1930 has the same buying power as $13.75 today. There's a calculator window, too. Let me put in $50,000, and see what comes up."

Nancy whistled. "Wow! That comes to $677,572.67! Keep in mind that this was only Sal's cut and that Ruby had already spent most of it. In the middle of the Great Depression that was a huge amount of money. No wonder why people were selling illegal whiskey and bathtub gin."

"It's a huge amount of money to me today, too. But does it belong to me? Can I get in trouble?

"I don't think so. Isn't there a statute of limitations or something? But did you notice that they are all silver and gold certificates? The government doesn't print money with silver and gold backing, anymore. These bills are worth more than their face value, actually."

"Really?" said Ivy. "But then, wouldn't I have to take it to a coin shop or coin show to sell them to a collector?"

Nancy bit her lip. "You're right. You could do that, but it would take a while because you could only exchange a small amount at a time, or it would bring too much attention to you."

They sat silently, trying to sort out the morality of keeping the discovery. Finally Nancy said, "Look, you really don't know where this money came from. You weren't there. You only know about it because Ruby told you, and she never saw the money exchange hands. Sal always made her go in the bedroom when the bootleggers were doing their transactions. So really, it's all speculation."

"I guess you could look at it that way. I just don't want to go to the hoosegow, as they used to say."

"Oh, Ivy, this money was earned, whether legally or illegally, over eighty years ago. It's impossible to trace it now. They didn't even know how to mark bills then, did they? And if it was from the sale of illegal booze, it came from many different sources, like dance halls, and speakeasies. Maybe even prostitution houses. I'd think you should just consider it your inheritance. Your GG wanted you to have it. That's why she told you where it was. Now what are you going to do with it?"

"I'm not sure, but it can't stay here."

"Hmmm." Nancy's wheels were turning. "I say," she said slowly, forming the plan as she talked, "you open several accounts at different banks, and make deposits of two thousand dollars at a time in each until most of it is gone. Make sure the numbers are always uneven, so it doesn't look suspicious."

"That will take a while, too."

"Yes, it could, but no one but us knows it's here, and I swear on my life, I will not even tell Matt. *Or* you could put it all in a safety deposit box which is totally secure and private, and only you will know what's in it. Then pull out however much you need a little at a time." Nancy was happy that the conversation of money had taken Ivy's mind off of Fox, if even for a short time.

"And that presents another problem, because I can't spend it. It's obvious these bills don't look like anything we know today. How could I ever spend it with arousing suspicion?"

Nancy's eyes lit up with a new idea. "You know how on some TV shows a person might hide money in a Swiss bank account? You could fly to Europe, and deposit it there in an account, then have some wired to your bank here when you need it. It's just numbers then and no longer traceable, plus you get a trip to Switzerland in the bargain."

"That might work. But I'm not sure it's legal to take that much cash out of the country. It would alert officials at the airport, wouldn't it? I'll have to think about this some more."

"Now, tell me, how will you spend this little fortune? You could take a nice vacation to someplace warm -- say you had been saving for a long time."

"No fun alone." Ivy's eyes filled up again.

Nancy berated herself for even coming close to the dangerous topic of Fox. Then her face lit up with an idea that was sure to perk up Ivy.

"Hey, you said you didn't have enough money to buy the cottage, but now you do. Why not wait for the house to go up for auction and bid on it yourself. Or buy it outright."

"Well, if I suddenly had money to buy it outright, people would surely be suspicious. And it will most likely sell for more than 50,000, anyway. I've already told the bank I have no savings, so I don't dare ask for a mortgage again. But yes," she said slowly thinking the plan through, "if I bid on it, out in the open, I'll be fine, because the public doesn't know my financial situation. I think auctions are cash only, so there would be no mortgage necessary. Once I figure out the best way to convert the bills, it will work. Nancy, you're a genius."

"Wouldn't it be nice to live in GG's cottage? You'd have your own little piece of paradise on White Lake right near the channel and Lake Michigan, and it's still a short drive to work."

"I would love that so much. It's almost too much to hope for. I'll go to my attorney tomorrow and ask if a family member is allowed to bid, but I'm sure they are. He can ask to be notified when the house comes up for auction." Some of Ivy's pain was lessening. Life wasn't all about having a man. She was perfectly capable of having a full life as a single woman. 'Who needs Fox, anyway?' she thought.

And then the text window lit up. She couldn't prevent herself from looking.

"I'm heading home. Won't be on this side of the state for a while. Please call me. I won't bother you

again. I'm sorry for whatever you think I did. I love you more than you know."

Ivy collapsed into her friends arms and sobbed. Her heart still yearned for Fox, but she would never trust him again.

Chapter Twenty-seven

Months later, Fox was heading back to Western Michigan from his home in Bay City. It was morning and already the day was promising to be a scorcher. He was driving with the top down in the hot July sun. He had cranked up the air conditioning in order to keep his body cool, but the top of his head was burning up. He reached for a ball cap on the seat next to him, not his usual head attire. His newly purchased summer fedora was out of reach on the floor behind him; he didn't want to risk losing it in the wind. As he drove to the Whitehall area, he thought of nothing and no one but Ivy. She had been in his thoughts every day since his last time here. And the nights – sleep was impossible, because whenever he closed his eyes he saw her face – laughing, teasing, and sexy. Oh, so sexy. He ached for her. Truly ached. He had heard of other people using that phrase, but never knew its true meaning until now. He wondered if he could ever get her back, but he had a plan, and if it worked, it might open the door for them to have a conversation. But who was he kidding? He wanted more than conversation; he wanted –

A horn honked at him, startling him out of his daydreaming. Apparently, he had drifted into another lane, and the driver was not too happy with him. The angry man passed him with a roar while flipping him the bird. Fox shrugged and mouthed 'I'm sorry.'

Today his trip had nothing to do with business, but it did have to do with real estate. He was going to the auction to place a bid on the Wabaningo cottage. It had taken some doing to make sure there was no conflict of interest. As soon as he had returned from his blowup with Ivy, he had begun making plans to salvage whatever they had. He wanted to do something so spectacular that it would force her to listen to him. So, with the agreement of his boss, he had paid for an outside person to do another appraisal. He explained to his boss that he had found a property that interested him, and that he had been wanting to own a cottage close to Lake Michigan. He planned to enter into the bidding along with any other interested party, but in order to avoid impropriety, he would prefer the appraisal be done by someone outside their firm and with whom he had never had contact before. His boss had agreed and said he was sure that was the only way he would have been allowed to bid, anyway.

And now the day for the auction had finally come. Fox had no idea how many people would be there as his competition, but he was going to get that house one way or another. As he pulled up to the property, he was disappointed to see several cars there already. People were milling about looking over the garage, boathouse, and dock. He saw one man looking up at the roof. A young couple exited the house talking excitedly; the man carried a computer tablet, while the woman had a paper tablet, one making notes while the other did calculations as to how much they thought the house was actually worth, and how much they could afford to put into it to bring it up to code. Fox had done all of his work ahead of time, since he had had the opportunity to do a thorough inspection previously. He had the numbers in his head, and the cash money he planned to spend was waiting in a duffle bag, locked away in his car. He was ready to go.

Ivy was the next to arrive, with Nancy at her side for support. She was more nervous than she had ever been, because getting this cottage meant so much to her. She was shocked at the turnout.

"Oh, Nance, look at all of the people. There's going to be way more competition than I thought."

"Yeah, I guess we should have expected that. Property on White Lake is highly desired. Even if they don't want the house, they're probably eager for the lot."

"I would sure hate to see someone tear it down for one of those modern monstrosities they've been building. I'll bet it was beautiful here when Ruby and Sal first owned it. They didn't have close neighbors then."

"And you still don't. That's one of the reasons this place will be in demand. It could be broken up into several lots. The money grubbers are hungry."

"Do you think we have a chance?" asked Ivy, already knowing the answer.

"It's a gamble, Ivy. No one ever knows at these things what people are willing to pay. Don't forget they have a budget, too, so we just have to hope that they don't exceed yours. Let's go sign up and get your number."

"I'm scared. I've never done this before." Nancy squeezed Ivy's hand with encouragement. It was then that the squeeze became tighter, as Ivy spotted the red Mazda with its top down. "It can't be, can it?"

As they neared the car, Ivy glanced in. A white fedora with a brown silk band sat carelessly on the floor in the back. Nancy noticed Ivy's face turn a pale shade and was afraid she was going to pass out.

"Come here, let's get out of the sun."

As they turned to find some shade, the women found themselves face-to-face with Fox. He stood there a moment trying to determine if she would be willing to talk. Would she make a scene? Would she ignore him? He smiled pleasantly.

"Excuse me, ladies, I was coming back for my hat."

There was an uncomfortable silence as Ivy glared at him, and then Nancy said, "Hi, Fox, I'm Nancy. I don't believe we've met." Thrilled to be acknowledged, Fox flashed the sexiest smile she had ever seen. His dark hair and eyes and his white teeth could have been right out of GQ magazine. Nancy had been told he was gorgeous, but until this moment she had no idea how charming and sexy he was. No wonder Ivy had fallen under his spell.

"Nice to meet you, Nancy. I'm Fox Marzetti. And how have you been, Ivy?" He waited to see what kind of response he would get, but all he received was a stony glare.

Ivy assumed Fox was there because of the appraisal for the State. She had no idea how these things worked and had never given a thought to the fact that she might run into him, or she would probably not have come. She yanked on Nancy's arm, tugging her away as they walked. Nancy looked at Fox, raised her eyebrows, and shrugged an 'I'm sorry.'

"Ivy, where are you going?" questioned Nancy.

"I'm leaving."

"But why in the world would you want to miss the chance to bid on the house? Stop and think. If you go, you'll only be punishing yourself."

They had reached the car and while Ivy was yanking on the handle, Nancy's words finally made their way through her anger. She sighed and collapsed behind the wheel. "You're right. I don't want to give him the satisfaction of getting away with it. He's probably just here to do his job, anyway; right?"

Nancy didn't want to point out that he had been holding a numbered paddle. "Of course. Let's get back with the others. I think they're about ready to start."

They worked their way into the group of about thirty people standing around in groups of twos and threes. Occasionally, there was a single person standing off to the side on their own. Ivy looked them over, wondering which one she would have to defeat in order to purchase her own house, the home that had been willed to her. The auctioneer stepped up on a small platform that had been brought in for the occasion. He had a stand in front of him and a gavel which he pounded to get everyone's attention.

"Is everyone ready to bid on this house? You already know the facts from the flyer that was sent out. It was built in 1929, is a three bedroom, two bathroom – the back bedroom and bathroom being added on in approximately 1950 or so. The rest has remained original and untouched. It would make anyone a fine summer cottage, and with a little work it could be updated to a four-season home. If you win the bid, you will be expected to pay in total before you leave the property. We accept cash or bank drafts only; no checks or money orders, please. The numbers I call out will be in the thousands, so to make sure there is no misunderstanding, if I call out thirty, it means thirty thousand dollars. The bidding will begin. Let's roll!" And with that he hit the gavel one time with force, making an echo through the trees, and started to talk faster than any human being should. The words rolled off his tongue sounding like a foreign language, but every once in a while Ivy heard numbers. She watched as people put up their paddles instead of calling out.

"Who will give me thirty?" Ivy was pleased with the starting point. It was a long way from the fifty thousand she had with her. Since she didn't have enough collateral for an unsecured loan without telling the bank about her cash, fifty thousand would have to be her limit; she had discovered a way to convert some of her cash, and she was now flush with legal money. After visiting several coin dealers and discreetly asking some questions about her bills, she was able to find one person who was willing to give her fifty thousand dollars for just five of the one-hundred-dollar gold certificates. Ivy was thrilled with the value of the bills. They made several different transactions on different days so each check he wrote would not be in a single large denomination. She was hoping that would protect her privacy and not alert a bank teller when she made her deposit. The rest of the money was stored in a safe deposit box until she could convert it at a later time. As far as the auction today, she had had to guess at what the house would go for, after researching online, so she had only brought the cash she had already converted.

One man jumped into the bid at the thirty thousand starting point. He was standing next to Fox, so she had no choice but to look in his direction. He was by far the most handsome man she had ever met, but good looks weren't everything. Trust was a big issue for Ivy, and that was completely gone now.

Ivy was jarred out of her thoughts when she heard the number forty. She decided she'd better jump in before it was too late. She raised her paddle, and was rewarded when she auctioneer pointed at her. But then another bid came in right at her heels – forty-five. A big jump. It was moving too quickly; the next denomination was forty-seven. Nancy poked her and she raised her paddle again. But before the auctioneer could call out a number someone yelled, "Forty-nine."

Fox saw the panic on Ivy's face. He had no idea she would bid on the house, but it made sense. She would want to try. He stood quietly, waiting for her to reach her limit. He would love nothing better than to see her win the house, so he would remain on the sidelines until it was necessary to take over. He was pleased when Ivy found her voice and yelled "Fifty." Immediately following someone countered with fifty-five. It broke his heart to see the look on her face. She was fighting back tears. He could wait no longer. Fox jumped in at sixty. He glanced sideways hoping to see her smile with pleasure, but she had turned beet red, her mouth set in a tight thin line. He had not known she was capable of such anger, even after what he had seen here at this house a few months ago.

The bidding went to sixty-seven, and then sixty-nine. Fox yelled "Seventy," and still the competitors bid. On and on and up and up with Fox fighting to stay in the game all the way to the end. He would not lose, no matter the cost. Ivy was stunned at the numbers. To her it was just a small rundown cottage that once belonged to her family. But others saw it differently. The double wooded lot, the lake and boathouse, all made a very attractive package and one that could be turned into real estate gold.

With the banging of the gavel, the hammer came down on the final bid of $100,000 -- twice what Ivy had been prepared to spend. Ivy was devastated to discover that the winner was Fox. How could he betray her like this? What kind of man was he? He actually had the nerve to look over at her with a huge grin of accomplishment and satisfaction.

Ivy marched over to him, now ready to fight. "Who are you, anyway?" she said loudly as others watched on. "Was this your plan all along? What sort of person does this?"

"Ivy, please. Let me explain." It seemed that that sentence should be set on replay, since that's all he could ever get out. She spun around and marched off to her car, with Nancy looking back over her shoulder once again.   He could see that Nancy felt some sympathy toward him. He would make an effort to go through her to get Ivy's attention, but not today. She was far too angry. He slowly walked over to the checkout table, paddle hanging low. Some of the others patted him on the back saying, 'Congratulations.' 'Great auction.' 'Good job.' 'You got a great piece of property.' But none of the praise mattered, because Ivy didn't care. He had just spent his life's savings on a house that would remain empty until he could offer it to the woman he loved.

Chapter Twenty-eight

"Are you sure you don't want me to drive?" asked Nancy, as the car spun away, and then careened around the curve faster than she was comfortable with.

"I'm fine. I'm just fine. *Perfectly* fine, as a matter of fact," spat Ivy.

"Well, maybe not, since your knuckles are turning white with that death grip on the steering wheel. It's not Fox's neck. Please slow down."

When Ivy glanced over at the look of fear on her friend's face, she relented and slowed the car down to a normal speed. "Sorry. I'm just so furious."

"I can see that. If you want my advice, and you probably don't, it's this: You have to let it go. It's over. You can't blame Fox, really."

"What? What are you talking about? He bought my house!"

"Yes, but if you noticed, he never placed a bid until he was sure you were out, and if it wasn't him, it would have been someone else who won the auction. You knew you had a slim chance of getting it with your small budget."

"I suppose you're right, but the thought of him living in GG's house just kills me. I would have preferred to imagine a family with children there -- someone I didn't know."

"I understand it's a loss, and it must feel awful. I mean you lost two grandmothers and a house all in one year, but Ivy, it's not the end of the world. You still have a lot of money. Think of the freedom that comes with that, if you're careful with it."

Ivy stopped for a stoplight, and as they waited for the light to turn green, she bit her lip thoughtfully. "Yes, you're right. But the house was worth more than its monetary value to me. I never planned on getting it after she passed, anyway. I had always assumed it would go to my father."

"And where was your father in all of this? He could have bid on it and easily paid way more than anyone else did."

"I've never known the whole story, but he wanted nothing to do with Olivia after he married his teenage bride. There must have been words spoken that could never be taken back."

The car began to roll slowly forward as the light turned green, following a car in front of them that seemed to have trouble getting started. "I don't mean to pry," said Nancy, "but whatever happened to Olivia's house?"

"Well, when Nana began to show signs of Alzheimer's, she moved to an assisted living facility. At that time she was perfectly capable of taking care of herself, but there were times when she would forget things, and so I talked her into moving. She wasn't happy about it at first, but I surely couldn't be there for her all the time, and we knew she would need more care in the future. There was always a fear that one day she would leave a burner on or get her meds mixed up. She still had savings at that time, but it finally became necessary to sell her house for the care. She couldn't get any Medicaid as long as she had assets. It didn't bother me, because I just wanted her to be taken care of properly. So basically, her house sold long before she died, and the equity went to the government."

"I get that someone has to pay back the government, it isn't free money, but what happens to people who have no assets?"

"They're covered, regardless, with no expectation of Medicaid Retrieval. That's the way the system works, good or bad. So, it's done." As they pulled into their apartment lot, Ivy maneuvered her car into her assigned garage. "Thank you, my friend, for sticking it out with me. I know I wasn't at my best today."

Nancy studied her best friend's dejected look. "You know, you didn't own a house yesterday, and you don't own one today. Nothing's changed. Go on with your life. Maybe someday you can buy a property on the lake or near it, if that's what you want. But don't let the anger hang around too long, or you'll become a bitter person."

"You're right --full of wisdom as always."

"Now, let's order some pizza. I'm starving. I have a bottle of wine chilling in my apartment."

Ivy laughed, because Nancy was always hungry and wine was just what she needed. Then she added, "Want to go back out and get a gallon of Moose Tracks ice cream, or Mackinac Island Fudge? Or do you prefer Bear Claw?" The girls laughed, because it had been their favorite debate lately over which Michigan flavor was the best. It felt good to laugh. Ivy was about to start a new chapter in her life, but Fox would never be a part of it.

Fox had signed the papers, and now held the keys in his hand, but his heart was heavy. He walked out to the dock after everyone was gone, and gazed out at the water. Last night he had had a vivid dream of Ivy. She was with him on this very dock, his arms wrapped around her protectively, as they slowly danced under the stars. A child was sleeping on a blanket in the grass. He could see a bright flash of something around her neck and hear the strains of music playing softly, as she sighed with happiness. The vision was so real, he had been certain it would come true. And if she would have given him a chance to explain, he was sure he could have convinced her to be his forever. But as it stood now, he would have to move mountains to get her to listen. Somehow, without knowing exactly what he had done wrong, he had crushed his love's heart, and in doing so had destroyed his own.

Chapter Twenty-nine

The September day was unseasonably warm, balmy almost. It looked and smelled more like spring, and with fear of losing the summer soon, people were out and about for their last chance to soak up the warm sun. In fact, it was a perfect day for a ride. It was the kind of day that made people happy, cheerfully saying "hello, how are you" or "let me get that door for you," to perfect strangers, or commenting, "It's a beautiful day, isn't it?" to someone in the parking lot. Ivy felt hopeful for the first time in a long time, since that July day, actually, when she had lost her house and her man at the same time. She had been feeling under the weather, most likely due to the change in the seasons, but today she was on top of the world. If no one was around, she might have burst into song, because last week in the mail, she had received the notice she had been waiting for. After only one submission, a publishing house was willing to publish her book, which she had simply named, 'Ruby and Sal.' They said it was a fresh look at Prohibition, and a different way to see those who were taking part in illegal operations, but were not always the bad guys portrayed in the movies. And they were especially interested in the love story. They actually used the words 'Hot.'

After Ivy had come out of her downer from not being able to buy the cottage, she had been convinced by Nancy to continue working on her story. Nancy pointed out that it was the only way she had left of staying close to her great-grandmother's past. She had taken the advice, which had been lovingly given, and after a little editing, she had sent a pdf of her manuscript to a publishing house. And here she was now, meeting with someone today about the details, after which she would take the contract to her attorney. So if all went according to plan, she could be a published author in a few months.

Suddenly, with the realization and excitement of accomplishing her dream, fear set in. Would Ivy be required to travel? Would she have to do book signings? Would there be interviews with the local news and others? All she had ever wanted was to be an author. She had never intended flying around the country to bookstore signings. What would she write on the inside covers? Did she have the personality for that kind of promotion?

It was a good thing she had been in a gas station quick stop when these thoughts had popped into her head, because she suddenly had to make a beeline for the restroom. Luck was with her, when she saw that no one else was in any of the stalls, because her retching and dry heaves had been rather embarrassing. By the time she had rinsed her mouth, she had begun to wonder if she really wanted to be famous. And with perfect clarity of thought, she knew the answer was no. Fame was not what she sought. She would have to see if there was a way to be published without all of the hoopla that went with it. This might be her one and only book. Isn't that what happened to the great Margaret Mitchell, author of Gone with the Wind? A 1937 Pulitzer Prize winner and then nothing. Poof! Ivy laughed to herself. Margaret was probably afraid of publicity, too, so at least she was in good company. And besides, she didn't have to worry about a Pulitzer Prize; that much she knew.

When Ivy stepped back outside, she took a deep breath of the wonderful fall air. It perked her up a little and gave her renewed energy. Her meeting was in a half hour, but after having a good talk with herself, she was now prepared to face the representative from the publisher. They would have demands, but so would she. She would not let anyone run over her. She straightened her shoulders, got in her car, and headed to the beginning of her new life.

As Fox pulled into the gas station, he saw Ivy getting in her car. His heart ached for her. He started to honk his horn, but stopped his hand in midair. She had not responded to any calls or texts in more than three months, now. He had to face the fact that it was over. But he was bound to run into her from time to time, because he planned on keeping his cottage, for a while at least, and she would most likely be in town sometimes when he was.

He was glad to see she looked happy. She seemed to have a spring in her step. Now he had to find a way to move on with his life, also. For now that meant pouring himself into his job throughout the week, and then on his days off, he worked on his lake house until he dropped.

Fox loved working with his hands, and was in fact, a very good handyman. Completing a job gave him a satisfaction that he never felt when he was appraising houses. There was something about standing back and looking at the physical evidence of his work at the end of the day. He thought it was probably primal, bred into a man's DNA since the beginning of time. So he felt perfectly confident in the changes he was planning to make to the cottage.

Today, after a run to the hardware store, he would begin scraping and painting the interior walls. He had already had a new roof professionally installed. It was easier to have it done that way while he was working on the other side of the state. It had to get finished before winter arrived, or he had been told he was going to have problems with heavy snow and leaks. He had already repaired some of the screening on the porch and replaced the steps, which had been rotting and were an accident waiting to happen. He had not yet slept in his house; tonight would be the first time. New locks were installed, and he had been assigned a new landline number. Cell phone service was sketchy out there, so a landline was still the safest way to go. His brother-in-law, Jarrod, was going to join him tomorrow, as he would need some help with the dock, and putting up some new dry wall. Once done with his cottage, he would have to make a determination whether he wanted to flip it, or keep it as a nice fishing retreat, but for now, he was enjoying the process.

An hour later, Fox arrived at his cottage. He had to admit to already having an attachment to it, something he had never felt for any house before. Most likely it was because it was part of Ivy. He would never forget seeing her look of disappointment when he bought it. He had never been able to talk to her about it, but he assumed she hadn't had the funds to bid any higher. Maybe someday – 'No,' he shook his head to clear it of an image that would never see the light of day.

"Time to get on with it, Fox, old boy," he said to himself.

Soon he was carrying boards, sheetrock, and gallons of paint inside. It had been a struggle to decide what colors to choose. Decorating was not his forte. He kept wondering what color Ivy would like, and in the end accidentally found himself buying colors that reminded him of her -- golden browns, soft yellows, and the cream of her complexion.

The kitchen granite was arriving today; he was anxious to see it in place. He had selected that one with the help of his sister, Joan. She said she didn't like anything too busy, so she had suggested a light brown with gentle swirls of gold. She was so pleased with her selection that he didn't have the heart to tell her it was the exact shade of Ivy's hair. He was having it installed by a professional, that being one job that was beyond his knowledge. So in order to stay out of the way, he would begin his own work in the master bedroom.

The walls in that room were in great shape. His biggest job was to tear off the wallpaper and prime it for paint. He would keep the bed for now. He rather liked the antique iron headboard. The mattress and box spring were old, probably had not been replaced in twenty years or more, but it would do until he could do some more shopping. He had purchased some fresh bedding – well, another sister, Anne, had bought it online for him. He thanked God for sisters.

≈

Fox was hard at work, when Ivy drove by. She had completed her meeting, which had gone much smoother than she had expected. No book signings were required for a new entry level book. Once it reached the top one hundred, they said they would begin a big push, but until then it was just too expensive to advertise in that way. So with the relief that came along with that revelation, Ivy had decided to take a nice drive along the lake, and naturally to Wabaningo. Fall outings to the cottage had always been a tradition for Ruby, Olivia, and Ivy. They all three loved the woods and lake in the fall, and there were always jobs that needed to be completed in order to put the cottage to rest for the winter. So to continue her routine, she decided to drive out there and just take a look. She wanted to see what the 'new owner' was doing with the place.

When she arrived, she drove slowly by, trying to take it all in. She was pleased to see the new roofing; it was a nice multi-color grey. And the porch had been spruced up a bit, too. Oh yes, there was a new exterior light next to the newly painted door – they were all things she had wanted to do, herself. Tears sprung to her eyes. Would she never get over losing this place?

It was obvious someone was working inside. There was a pickup truck outside, and she could hear music coming from within. Afraid to get caught looking, she let her car continue to roll forward.

Was it Fox? Was he with a new woman? Were they planning on moving in? The thought of him being with another woman in her house was unbearable, but of course, he was a healthy American male. He wouldn't be alone for long.

As Ivy continued past the house, Fox stepped outside to grab a hammer that he had left in the back of the truck. He jerked his head up at the sound of the motor going by, instinct pulling him in that direction. Was that Ivy's car? No, it couldn't be. She would never risk coming out here and running into him, he knew that much. It must be wishful thinking. He shrugged. "Back to work, dude," he said to himself.

Heading straight back to his work in the bedroom, Fox walked over the old rug, as he had done many times today, but this time he heard a squeak he had not noticed before. Wondering if there was a loose board he should take care of, he lifted the rug and stepped on the area again. Upon a closer look, he could tell that one particular board *was* loose, but not only loose, it actually looked like a different color, as if it had been replaced at one time. He grabbed his screw driver, and inserting it into the crack, he gently lifted. The board came right up, and he was surprised to find an opening which had most likely been used to store something, perhaps valuables – a hiding place. This house had only had one owner, as far as he knew, but it was almost ninety years old. In a time when banks were not used as often as they are now, it probably held the owner's cash.

The thought of cash reminded him of something Ivy had said on the day he had come to appraise the house, which had made no sense at the time. Something about Prohibition, and a necklace. He thought that's what she had said, when he had come upon her downstairs by that old safe. If they had a safe, he wondered, why would they need a loose board hiding place? Upon placing his hand on the loose board again, he suddenly felt a very strong urge to go back down to the cellar. He wanted to get down there before the workmen came. He needed to get there, *now*.

He had removed the rug and table last week; they were too old to be of any use to him. With an easy tug, he was able to lift the door in the floor, and lower himself to the dark, dank room. His sense of adventure was on high alert, as he turned the beam around the small room. The safe door was still open as it had been on that day. He panned the shelves and miscellaneous items, until his beam came to rest on an area that looked different than the other walls. Why had he not noticed this before? What kind of appraiser was he?

Three of the rounded sides were rock, but the one in the back was cement block. Something had been sealed up. It was either because the rocks had deteriorated, their seals leaking in moisture, or there was an opening that someone wanted blocked. He ran his hands over the joints. Some of the mortar had loosened. It would not be a difficult for two men to break through it. If he could contain himself and wait until Jarrod came tomorrow, he could ask him to help. Knowing his brother-in-law, he would probably much prefer doing demolition than putting up drywall, anyway.

He heard someone call out from above. The granite guys had arrived. He quickly scrambled up, and closed the door. He would prefer that no one else knew about his discovery.

"Come on in, guys," he called. "I was just down in the fruit cellar. Let's get started."

Chapter Thirty

The thunder rumbled and the lightning cracked as the night slowly dragged by. Fox tossed and turned in the old iron bed, as he anxiously awaited for morning. Thoughts of what he might find behind that cement wall kept rolling around in his head. And Ivy's words when he had found her in the cellar by the safe were almost screaming at him in the dark – prohibition, necklace, my cottage, betrayed.

On the few occasions he had fallen asleep, his vivid dreams portrayed a beautiful woman with flashing eyes and a sparkling piece of jewelry around her neck. The woman was a stranger to him, but at times she morphed into Ivy in the way that dreams sometimes do. He saw himself wearing his summer hat, planted jauntily on the back of his head, while she was in a sheer nightie. He could see her lovely shape and the dark circles on her breasts as she twirled to music, completely uninhibited. She was dancing just for him, and he was intoxicated with the vision before him. He reached out to pull her to him, but she elusively moved away, laughing as she did so; her flirtatious teasing was meant to arouse him. A brilliant red and white sparkle kept flashing in his eyes. It had a kaleidoscope effect as the rainbows moved over his face. He slowly stood up and this time was able to pull her into his arms -- her warmth and scent, so familiar. He buried his nose in her neck and sighed, promising to never do anything to hurt her, to love her forever, and cherish her with all of his heart.

"Ivy," he whispered. "Ivy."

Fox woke with her name on his lips, wondering what he could do to get her back. He needed her for life, his very existence depended on her loving him. He must have fallen back into a deep sleep, because the next thing he knew there was a loud pounding on the door.

"Hey, are you in there, dude? It's me, Jarrod."

Fox jumped up so quickly, he found himself entangled in the sheets and almost fell to the floor. He yanked on his jeans, while hopping on one foot, and yelled, "I'm coming."

He padded to the door, barefoot, while rubbing a hand over his morning facial shadow. Opening the door for his brother-in-law, he sheepishly said, "Sorry, man. I overslept, I guess."

"Hey," Jarrod teased, "I got an early start and drove all this way just for you. You sounded so anxious for me to come when we talked last night, and now I find you still in bed like Sleeping Beauty, or something." Jarrod stepped inside and took off his rain soaked jacket. He lightly tossed it over a chair, but Fox was right behind him to retrieve it and hang it on a peg by the door.

"Didn't my sister teach you anything, you Neanderthal?"

"Yeah, sorry, I thought this was going to be a bachelor pad."

Fox laughed at Jarrod's embarrassment. "No problem." He slapped him playfully on the back. "I didn't want the dripping water to get on my new hardwood floors, is all."

"Got any coffee?" asked Jarrod, hopefully.

"Oops, I had planned to have it all done when you arrived, but, well you know –

"Yeah, lazy bones didn't get up in time."

"I'll get it started right now," replied Fox, working efficiently at the sink. "We can talk while we wait for it to perk."

"Yeah, what's with the mystery?"

"Well, I made a discovery yesterday that had me pretty excited. You know how I love to seek out Al Capone's houses in Michigan."

"Sure do and so does everyone else in the family. You're a little obsessed. That's all we hear about at the dinner table."

"I wouldn't say that."

"Oh, I would."

"Okay, well, this time I think I really have something. And you get to be in on the discovery."

"Well, tell me. Spit it out."

Fox grinned, unable to contain his story any longer. "Yesterday, when I was down in the root cellar, or fruit cellar, whatever you want to call it, I noticed a wall that was different than the others."

"How so?" With his interest piqued, Jarrod sat forward. Despite his teasing, he had always been just as fascinated with tales of Al Capone owning houses all over Western Michigan as Fox.

"Three of the walls are all stone, a real old Michigan cellar, but the third side has a section that has been blocked in."

"You mean cement blocks?"

"Yes, and it's sort of in a square pattern. I'm thinking that there's either a room hidden behind there, or possibly a tunnel like so many homes have discovered."

"Cool! What are your plans?"

"You and I are knocking that baby down today. You did bring the sledge hammers I texted you about; right?"

"Sure did. When can we get started? This is right up my alley."

"I figured it would be, you big brute. Let's have some coffee, then head down below."

Jarrod was thrilled with being in on Fox's demolition job. He loved nothing better than knocking things down and tearing them apart.

After Jarrod brought in the heavy hammers and tossed them down the opening, and as soon as the first cup of coffee was consumed, they carefully lowered themselves down the ladder steps, lanterns in hand. Fox was just as thrilled with the sight of the wall as he had been last night, and Jarrod was coming unglued, as he liked to say.

"Okay, we are both holding sledge hammers. With a knuckle-head like you, this could be dangerous," said Fox. "You start on that side, and I'll be over here. We don't want to hit each other with a blow from one of these babies. My sister would kill me if I killed you. Let's do alternating strikes. You go first."

Jarrod grinned like a little boy seeing his brand new bike at Christmas. He took a strong blow; some mortar vibrated and crumbled. With each strike after that, it became easier to free the blocks. As soon as the first six were removed, both men peeked inside, holding a lantern up and shot their flashlight beams inside. They high-fived each other once it was obvious that it looked like a hallway on the other side.

"You're right, Fox. I think it's a tunnel."

"Let's keep going until the opening is big enough for us to get inside."

"You got it." And with that he took a swing so hard several blocks fell at the same time.

In just a few minutes more the men were crawling through the opening, and once on the other side, panting hard with their efforts, they stopped to hold the lanterns up and get a good look around.

"Yes! It's a tunnel. I knew it!" exclaimed Fox. "Is it possible I own my very own Al Capone house?"

Jarrod was already moving down the walkway. "Let's find out."

In a short amount of time they came to another set of ladder steps. Jarrod stepped back so Fox could go up first. "It's your house. You do the honors."

Fox climbed carefully, aware that the steps could give at any time. Once at the top he lifted a heavy door on hinges. And when he poked his head through, he was thrilled to see that he was in the middle of the garage. Luckily for him, there was nothing over the opening, so he went up, opening the hatch all the way, which allowed Jarrod to follow him.

"This is perfect."

"What is?" asked Jarrod as he reached the top.

"It's an obvious escape route. The bootleggers would have pulled up to the garage if they were being chased. They would leave their car in front of the garage door and hurry down the steps, as someone pushed the car over the hatch door. The move was so common, it was a wonder the Feds never caught on."

"Wow, this is amazing. But I noticed the tunnel went even further," added Jarrod.

"Come on. I think I know where it leads."

Like two little boys on a treasure hunt, the grown men scrambled down the steps eager to see the next path they would travel. After walking for a few minutes, brushing away cobwebs as they went, they came to another set of steps. Fox stepped back and smiled at Jarrod.

"After you," he said with a bow, like royalty.

"Me?"

"You've earned it."

"Thanks, man." Jarrod bounced up the steps so fast, that Fox had to warn him they might not be safe. But it turned out they were as solid as a brick. When Jarrod got to the top and attempted to open the hatch, it wouldn't budge. After a lot of pushing, he finally got it to open just a crack, enough so he could see just a bit of where he might be.

"What do you see?"

"I think there's something on top of us. That's why I can't get the door open all the way. It looks like it might be inside another building. I see some tarps, and a dirt floor, but that's all I can get. I'm basically looking at the floor."

"Come on," called Fox. "Follow me. I'm pretty sure I know where this is. I might need your help."

They grabbed their lights once again and ran through the tunnel, climbing up the steps to the kitchen in seconds.

"Grab your coat, I think it's still raining. Do you mind if your work boots get wet?"

"That's what they're for. Let's go!"

They dodged the rain as Fox led the way to the boathouse, and once inside, Fox was pleased to see that underneath the fishing boat that had been left behind, was a large grease-stained rug. "We need to push this boat back a bit."

"Okay, release the brake on the trailer."

Then with a grunt and a shove, the boat was rolled partially out the door.

"We got it," yelled Fox. "The rug is exposed enough so we can look underneath."

Upon lifting the rug, they were rewarded with another hatch, the very one Jarrod had tried to raise from below. When they looked inside, they were confident they were at the end of the tunnel.

Jarrod pulled his head up out of the hole, dirty and sweaty, and said, "So, tell me. How would they have used this?"

"I'm now 100% positive that this was used for bootlegging. Think of it. It's a perfect spot. The hooch was purchased from the Purple Gang along 131 which was the dividing line between the two gangs. There was probably a specified way station. It would have been driven here, and unloaded into the tunnel through the garage and then carted down to the boathouse to make sure no neighbors ever saw their activity. From there it was loaded onto a small boat and taken through White Lake, and then out the channel to Lake Michigan where a larger boat would be waiting to take the illegal alcohol to Chicago. A lot of money must have passed through hands, here, which would explain the large safe."

"So who owned this house? Do you have any idea?" Fox had never confided in any family members about Ivy. They had an idea that he was seeing someone on the West side, maybe someone special, but he had refused to talk about it, and after a few moody responses, they had left the subject alone.

"I have a very good idea. I think it's time I tell you a story. Let's go back into the house, clean up a bit, and get something to eat."

After pushing the boat back into its original position, the two men walked back to the house in the slow gentle drizzle. Once inside, dry and warm, Fox told everything he thought was pertinent. How he had met Ivy, the day at the lighthouse, their indoor picnic, and without going into details, he inferred how their romance had developed. His eyes had a sparkle, and he couldn't stop smiling as he recounted their walk in the rain and then how they had spent the rest of the day and night at her place. And as he came to the part where he had later discovered her at a house he was to appraise, not knowing it belonged to her family, and then how he had bid on the house at the auction, and how much he had hurt her, Jarrod watched as his whole body crumbled with the pain of what he had done.

"That's too bad, Fox. I feel for you. Can you get her back?"

"I've tried but she'll have nothing to do with me. I even went to her work one day, and then changed my mind as I realized that she might think of it as stalking. She's normally a gentle, caring person, but she is furious with me. I don't think it can be undone."

"But you know what our discovery means? Her family was involved in prohibition in some way. I think you need to do research on the original owner of this house. It might actually be Al Capone himself."

"Most likely, not. He only bought two houses in his own name, and they're both accounted for. He had friends and loyal devotees who would harbor him and cover for him wherever he went. This cottage could be one of those places."

"Okay," said Jarrod, with sudden clarity. "Let's keep working on the house, and then maybe sometime in the future, you'll be able to bring her out here and see what you've done. Until that time, it *does* belong to you. And if it had not been you, it would have been someone she wouldn't have known, at all. So at the very least, she still has a connection, here."

"Yeah, good or bad, right?"

The men finished their meal and continued to work the rest of the day. They made a lot of progress on the bedroom, and as soon as the rain stopped they were able to drag the dock to the shore and cover it with a tarp in preparation for winter. Jarrod left late that night, even though Fox had encouraged him to stay over. He said he had to get home for his oldest son's ballgame in the morning, but he promised to come back and help whenever Fox needed him. As he drove away,

Fox realized how blessed he was to have such a wonderful family. Not only were his sisters the best, but their husbands were, too. Just knowing that someone would always be there for him was a comfort. That was something not all men could say of their families.

As soon as Jarrod left, Fox turned off the lights and went to bed early. After the day's activities, he was so exhausted that he fell asleep immediately. Once again, he had dreams of an unknown dancing girl whose image turned into Ivy. In a blurry haze, he could see Ivy was dancing with him on the dock, slow and sensual, with her body pressed tightly to his. When they came inside, to the warm glow of the fire, he took her to his bed; and all during their lovemaking, red and crystal lights skipped gently over her breasts. When Fox woke in the morning, he was bathed in sweat. This house was telling him something. He knew it. He had had dreams of women before, sexy dreams at that, but nothing like this. This seemed so real, and yet he couldn't quite see it all.

As soon as he was finished with his breakfast, he went down into the cellar once more. He wanted to take another look at the tunnel and see if he had missed something. When his eyes lighted on the safe, his heart skipped a beat. The safe door was open and had been when he had found Ivy down there that day; but had it always been open? Had Ivy found the combination and been looking for something? He studied the dust on the safe. The top and sides were thick with an old layer of grime. It was untouched. There were no fingerprints whatsoever, but when he swung the heavy door back, careful to not let it close, he could see where someone had brushed off the gilt lettering, and there were smudges around the lock. She had unlocked it, that much was certain, and she had been trying to protect it from being seen by him. The interior shelves were empty, but he now distinctly remembered that she had come up the stairs with nothing in her hands.

Fox squatted down in front of the safe and ran his hands all over the interior. Nothing unusual there. It was solid. Then he leaned over the back as far as he could and with the glow of the flashlight shining down, he looked into the dark space behind. Nothing. Not willing to give up, Fox got down on all fours and tried to peer under the safe. It was raised off the ground by the heavy iron wheels, so there was a five- to six-inch clearance. Unless he placed his cheek on the dirt floor he couldn't see underneath, so he ran his hands under the edge as far back as he could reach. When he touched something soft like fabric, he gasped. He wiggled his fingers, cursing his large hands. A woman would have had a much easier time of it. Finally, he was able to grab ahold of a corner of the cloth and tug.

It came away easily. Fox smiled with satisfaction, and sat back on his heels to look at his find. It was a small bag made of a burlap-type cloth. It was dirty but still intact. There was something inside; he could feel a bumpy surface through the fabric. Feeling the cold and damp seep through his pants, he decided to stand before the unveiling.

As he slowly extracted the wrapped parcel, his hands began to shake. A red flash caught his eye. He felt a warmth spread throughout his whole body. In his hands, he held the most beautiful piece of jewelry he had ever seen in his life. A ruby and diamond necklace. There was no doubt as to the fact that the gems were real. They caught the light of the lantern and almost glowed. And then a hazy vision came to him of a girl dancing in the moonlight, and once again he saw Ivy in her place. Was this what she had been looking for?

"Ivy," he simply said, with a yearning far stronger than anything he had felt before. "Ivy," he called, as a tear rolled down his face.

At that exact moment, Ivy was waking up from a dream-filled sleep. She quickly sat up in bed as she felt a warmth spread around her neck. She gasped and placed a hand there, as if to protect something -- and then, she fainted.

Continue the story of Fox and Ivy in

Maisy and Max, Book 2
of The Unforgettables
view an excerpt following Author's Notes

Author's Notes

When I started this series, I began by looking into all of the famous and infamous people who were either born in Michigan or had connections to Michigan in some way. And of course, Al Capone was the first one I thought of. He, no doubt, has the most fact and fiction surrounding his name in this area of anyone. But the facts are that Al Capone did have hiding houses spread throughout West Michigan. And the facts are that he never put them in his name. To this date there are only two houses that have ever been discovered to have had a deed with his name on it; one is in Escanaba, Michigan, and the other is in Palm Island, Florida, where he retired after his early release from prison in 1939 for, ironically, good behavior.

It is thought that he was the mastermind for the St. Valentine's Massacre in 1929 in Chicago, but since he was in Florida at the time, nothing could ever be pinned on him. It is very possible, though, that he hired The Purple Gang from Michigan to take out his nemesis Bugs Moran, head of The North Street Gang. He failed to get Moran, as he was not there that day, but a big share of his head men were gunned down.

There are many houses along the shoreline, inland, and deep in the woods that have discovered tunnels, all claiming to be part Al Capone's operation. One of those houses is in the county that I now live in. It's a bed and breakfast now in downtown Newaygo. A tunnel ran from the house which was owned by Al Capone's attorney, to a bar across the street. The local museum has an Al Capone display running at the time of this writing.

Although White Lake, and its channel to Lake Michigan is a perfect setup for any bootlegging operation, it is one hundred percent all my imagination. The area called Wabaningo and the city of Whitehall do exist, but if there ever was any illegal rum-running going on there, I have never been told of it.

All characters are fiction, except for Al Capone, of course, so please don't annoy the neighbors on White Lake looking for a house that does not exist.

I hope you enjoyed the first installment of The Unforgettables and will continue to read the story of Ivy and Fox with Book Two called Maisy and Max. Thank you for following me, and giving me encouragement to continue on with my writing. I would really appreciate it if you would leave a review on Amazon or Goodreads.

Here are some of the links to my Internet research:

www.onewal.com/a017/f_swmichigan.html

www.9and10news.com/story/25276631/special-report-petoskey-underground

www.lostinmicigan.net/notorious-purple-gangconnections-mid-michigan

www.bigstarlakehistory.com/capone.htm

www.99wfmk.com/caponemichigan

http://www.wzzm13.com/news/local/michigan
-life/al-capones-gun-to-be-auctioned-off-in-west-
michigan/370154654

http://www.mafiahistory.us/a017/f_swmichiga
n.html

Maisy and Max

Prologue, 1889–1890

Edward was eager to leave London. The circus had been here almost two months, since the beginning of November, and even though the weather had been a little more agreeable the last few days, it was still cold and damp. He was told the temperatures would continue to climb away from the 5-7 degrees Celsius it had been hovering at, but numbers didn't really matter when you were cold. Cold was cold. He was looking forward to the crossing to New York, and then P.T. Barnum would take its winter break in Connecticut, before starting on their scheduled route again in April. Edward didn't usually mind traveling, but this year it had been wearing on him a little more than it usually did at the end of the season. The extended months for the European tour had been difficult. Maybe it was because he was without a mate. A nice woman would have done wonders to keep him warm at night, and the companionship would have been a whole lot better than the roustabouts he usually chummed with. The simple fact was that Edward was growing up and ready to settle down, something he never would have thought about himself in a million years.

A walk in the rain was probably a bad idea, but Edward needed some time alone. He had to think about his future and ponder what was to become of him if he ever left the circus life. He roamed from street to street, each one more dismal than the last. London was a dark and dreary place in the 1890s, especially if you were poor. He stopped for a minute to look around and get his bearings, trying to decide if he was lost, when a shop window decorated with brightly colored scarves caught his eye. The festivity reminded him of circus colors meant to attract attention. He crossed the street to see what it was about, and as he drew near he could read the letters painted on the glass -- *Fortune Telling. See Your Future.* Edward smiled to himself because they had the same type of fortune tellers at the circus, and he knew they were all a sham. He had been in on some of the shake downs himself, helping poor souls who only wanted some answers to feel better about themselves. Some marks were more difficult than others, but they all caved eventually. Out of curiosity as to how they did things here in England, he entered. His experience would be good for a laugh when he retold it back at the grounds.

A small bell tinkled when he opened the door, and shortly after a striking woman dressed in a turban and a long loose kaftan came to greet him. Her makeup was exaggerated, and she wore an excess of jewelry – huge gold hoops in her ears, and several necklaces around her neck. The colors of the gems flashed in the light. Her expression was blank as she beckoned him to come behind the curtain of beads; the bracelets on her wrist clinked pleasantly with the movement of her hand. Edward smiled to himself when he saw the traditional crystal globe on the table with a burning candle beside it. It was exactly the way the circus fortune teller was set up, but when he sat down across from her, he felt the hairs on his arms stand up.

"So, you want to know your fortune?" she asked in a sultry tone, as she leaned forward and stared directly into his eyes.

"Uh, yes," said Edward. He was a little shaken, and he had no idea why -- he knew the drill. "I am trying to make a decision, and I thought I could use some help."

There was silence as she studied him, making him feel very uncomfortable. "You want a mate?" she asked in her thick accent. "Yes, I can see it clearly."

Edward wondered if she was trying to sell herself to him. He turned a deep shade of red. She laughed making him feel embarrassed; he was not an innocent child; he had had experiences – just not any kind of permanent relationship. "Yes, actually," he stuttered. "Perhaps, I am looking for a wife."

She smiled for the first time. "Now we are getting somewhere. Give me your hands." Edward reached across the table and took both her hands in his – she gasped, and pulled back.

"What? What happened?" he asked.

"I think you are a very special man. I think you are the one I have been waiting for."

"What do you mean?"

She reached up to her neck an unclasped what looked like a ruby and diamond necklace, but as he well knew, it was the same kind of fake paste that all the circus performers wore. She wrapped it around her fingers and closed her eyes, then she took his hands into hers once again, with the necklace touching them both. Edward felt a warmth and tingle right down to his toes. He smiled, relaxed and closed his eyes; it felt like home, it felt like comfort; it felt like love.

"What is your name?" she softly asked.

"Edward. Edward Woods."

Her eyes widened. "You are Gypsy? You speak Romany?"

"No, I don't speak Romany, but I have been told that my ancestors are Romani from Wales."

"Of course you are. So I thought. Here, take this." She separated her hands from his and pushed the necklace into his hands alone.

"Why?" Edward was completely puzzled. He had come here for a reading, not a piece of jewelry.

"This necklace has special powers. It has been waiting many years for you. It wants to be with you and you only. It will bring you the answers you need, and when you know the time is right, you will pass it on to the one you love and receive wondrous results." Then she smiled a very seductive smile. "Would you like to try it out?"

Edward did not have a clue what she was talking about, and beautiful as she was, he had no intention of doing what he was sure she was suggesting. Besides he couldn't afford to buy the necklace, anyway. After last night's card game, he was flat broke.

She laughed out loud, as she read his mind. "No, there is no need to pay me for the bauble. It is yours, as it should be. I have only been the caretaker. It is my pleasure to find the rightful owner. Now, go and find your woman; she will be much more eager than I."

Made in the USA
Middletown, DE
07 November 2020